To Ma

Hope yo   o J

Gertrude

x x x

PURE
SLUSH
BOOKS

PURE
SLUSH
BOOKS

THe TYRaNNy oF BACoN

PURE SLUSH VOL. 18

First published as a collection August 2020
Content copyright © Pure Slush Books and individual authors
Edited by Matt Potter

BP#00093

All rights reserved by the authors and publisher. Except for brief
excerpts used for review or scholarly purposes, no part of this book
may be reproduced in any manner whatsoever without express
written consent of the publisher and the author/s.

Pure Slush Books
32 Meredith Street
Sefton Park SA 5083
Australia

Email: edpureslush@live.com.au
Website: https://pureslush.com/
Store: https://pureslush.com/store/

Original cover photo copyright © Bas Silderhuis
Cover design copyright © Matt Potter

ISBN: 978−1−922427−02−1

Also available as an eBook
ISBN: 978−1−922427−03−8

A note on differences in punctuation and spelling

Pure Slush Books proudly features writers from all over the English−speaking world.
Some speak and write English as their first language, while for others, it's their second
or third or even fourth language. Naturally, across all versions of English, there are
differences in punctuation and spelling, and even in meaning. These differences are
reflected in the work *Pure Slush Books* publishes, and they account for any
differences in punctuation, spelling and meaning found within these pages.

Pure Slush Books is a member of the
Bequem Publishing collective
http://www.bequempublishing.com/

• Alex Reece ABBOTT • Tobi ALFIER • Jane ANDREWS •
• Helen M. ASTERIS • Cathie AYLMER • D. A. BAILEY •
• Linda BARRETT • Paul BECKMAN •
• Cheryl Ferguson BERNINI • Steven BORG • John BOST •
• Sy BRAND • Mark BRIDGE • Laurie BYRO •
• J.D. CARTER • Patti CASSIDY • Chuka Susan CHESNEY •
• Jan CHRONISTER • Michael CIESLAK • Jennifer CLARK •
• Robert COOPERMAN • Carolyn CORDON •
• Matt COWAN • Ruth Z. DEMING • Julius DE SMEDT •
• Steven DEUTSCH • Tom FEGAN • James FITZGIBBON •
• AJ FOWLER • Nod GHOSH • Michael GIGANDET •
• Ken GOSSE • Jonnie GUERNSEY •
• Samuel GULLIKSSON • Tom HAZUKA •
• Mark HEATHCOTE • Sharron HOUGH •
• Mark HUDSON • Abha IYENGAR • Doug JACQUIER •
• Tim JARVIS • Paul JAUREGUI • Jessica JOY •
• Sarah Jane JUSTICE • Kathleen KENNY • Len KUNTZ •
• John LANE • Tracie LARK • Christine LAW •
• Mike LEWIS-BECK • Ann LISKA • Lisa Marie LOPEZ •
• John MASKEY • Holly McCANN • Jan McCARTHY •
• Lynda McMAHON • Gwendolyn Joyce MINTZ •
• Colleen MOYNE • Remngton MURPHY • John NOTLEY •
• Jill OLSON • Daniel O'DONOVAN •
• Eileen O'REILLY • Carl 'Papa' PALMER •
• Winston PLOWES • Matt POTTER • Niles REDDICK •
• Alex ROBERTSON • Eve ROSE • Jennifer ROSE •
• Ruth Sabath ROSENTHAL • Leah Holbrook SACKETT •
• Kathryn SADAKIERKSI • Gerard SARNAT •
• Wayne SCHEER • Iris N. SCHWARTZ •
• Andrew SELLORS • Mir-Yashar SEYEDBAGHERI •
• Martin SHAW • Jonathan SLUSHER • E. M. STORMO •
• Christopher TATTERSALL • Lucy TYRRELL •
• Alan WALOWITZ • Gertrude WALSH •
• Michael WEBB • Hazel WHITEHEAD • Debbie WIESS •
• Allan J. WILLS • Rita WILSON •

"It's like there's this tyranny of bacon!"

Uttered by editor Matt Potter
while sitting at a café on Semaphore Road,
after throwing down the menu in disgust
at the inclusion of bacon (which he
doesn't like much) in every dish
that even vaguely appealed to him.

Contents

Poetry

Poetry

Bacon in Coronavirus Times

Linda Barrett

Supermarket shopping:
Don my face mask
hands in latex gloves
a six—foot long distance from
Next—door neighbors
The shelves are bare:
Milk, toilet paper, and bottled water
Gone like Kobe Bryant
Seven varieties of bacon left
At least social isolation is good.

Leaving Scandia

Mike Lewis–Beck

Off the breakfast board I scooped two white eggs,
soft–boiled but boiled one minute too long
I learned, capping them with my table knife.

Looking up from an egg cup I watched
a toddler struggling to mount his Trip–Trap
high chair, wanting help, like my sons did.

The coffee was off, made from a button
machine—quick, quiet, no taste. The bacon
I left in its pile, a tangled mess of garters.

Early light, for the Copenhagen flight,
I wheeled my Samsonite case to the bus,
took a window seat, counted pigeons

pecking crumbs, second–time lovers pecking
cheeks, parting so sweet, she a svelte brunette
like Audrey Hepburn, even to the blue–belted raincoat.

My head bubbling about the gold band
on her right—hand burst when I heard a scream—
"Let me fucking go!"

in several languages— a lipsticked teen,
black braid twisting, cream face flushing
as she wrestled the police.

The bus pulls away, its blue body lurches.
Yellow fields of rapeseed unfold, as in a Van Gogh.
I read a story about old men, and doze.

Dinner Plans

Ruth Sabath Rosenthal

Watching a co-worker of mine
approaching the candy machine
licking his chops —
two of his sidekicks
already there pitching foul
to a wee bird
of a new girl in the office
jars my memory
of my first job
& wakens the dormant craw
deep in my throat
A lout had stuck his snout
in my personal affairs
& made me the butt
of his ridicule &
laughing stock
of the office staff —
that flashback
thrusting me onto the brink
of heaving my lunch
at the three slovenly musketeers

by now having reduced the poor girl to tears
prompts a more therapeutic urge in me
thus fully downsizing my upchuck —
I'll fry up some bacon
& eggs for dinner
& while the lip—smack'n strips
are crisping
just to the verge of char
I'll toast the swine
with a pint or two
each swill a permanent nail
skewered through
their nasty tales & proverbial butts
I'll graphically illustrate
in my popular daily blog
& post it sometime
before the office opens tomorrow
making sure to send a text alert
(accompanied by a slew of piggy emojis)
to everyone at work but
the actual swine themselves

Epitaffy for a Singing Telegrapher

Ken Gosse

His final verse, an epigram,
he cyphered in a diagram,
then sent himself by telegram—
well−sung from robust diaphragm—
a witness to his final laugh,
recorded for his epitaph.

At short last he was supersized,
and though no others were surprised
'twas far too late he realized
the fate which he himself devised
from food which he idealized.
The coroner wrote "baconized".

When they laid him in the earth,
his headstone suffered not a dearth
of room to tell, with touch of mirth,
gourmandic pleasures since his birth,
for in the end his final girth
would far exceed his height's net worth.

Pioneer

Kathryn Sadakierski

Sizzling on the stove,
Bacon is a symphony for the ears,
A feast for the eyes,
For some.

Stirred into ice cream, garnishing cupcakes,
Bacon is a valuable currency,
Part of every meal
Carnivorous gastronomists devour greedily.
A commodity, it has become
Everything,
The porcine delicacy
Causing individuals to push aside calories
In favor of sumptuous bliss.

Valentines are laced with maudlin messages,
The latest of which
Is "don't go 'bacon' my heart,"
Expressing love
From the depths of the heart, and further yet,
The stomach,
No thought given to Upton Sinclair,
And the jungle's ready—made dinners.

Bacon is a cultural phenomenon,
No longer just a dish,
But rather, nourishment
For the primal dreams of humanity.

Still? I don't see it.
How can you not like bacon?!
They all have asked me,
As I nibble on my plate of veggies.
Perhaps I've seen too many grassroots food movies,
Or maybe it's just
That I've never had much of a taste for meat,
But bacon's tyranny
Has not subjected me.

Bacon is hearty,
And for some Americans,
A nod to Paul Bunyan and Jacksonian democracy,
With a pull—yourself—up—by—the—bootstraps,
Make—your—own—luck mentality,
Symbolizing determination,
The pioneer spirit,
Fed by the meal that most epitomizes
Strength, rugged frontier pluck and grit,
Brawn without beef,

Bacon
Is a link to past history,
The fabric of national ancestry,
(Or at least
What it is supposed to be)
In tall—tale imagery,
Telling people, in times of uncertainty,
About who they can presently be.

Bacon may not be the key,
But it says something about a people's identity,
The lens through which they see,
Though my bacon—less palate
May tell a different story.

Bacon

Robert Cooperman

There used to be this commercial
for "Bacon Bits" dog biscuits:
the golden retriever in a frenzy
at the aroma wafting from the box.

"What does it say? What does it say?"
its frantic cry, "I'm a dog, I can't read!"
The commercial always cracked us up.

I felt that frustration growing up kosher;
bacon in our apartment? Blasphemy!
So on Sunday mornings, on my way
to buy the paper, bagels and lox
for our family's leisurely breakfast,
I'd linger outside Mrs. Cohen's door,
hoping my buddy Jay would sense me
at the gates of paradise and invite me in.

Well, a kid could dream.

But when our parents were on a saved—for
tour of Spain, my brother and I fried some up,
and as Jeff always raves, "Oh baby!"
We practically saw Jesus and converted,
so we could eat bacon daily.

But for the next three days, we kept
the kitchen window thrown open
in frigid February, the fan blowing
the perfume out; we scrubbed the skillet
as if our lives depended on
removing all traces of that bouquet.

After our parents returned home, hugged us,
and gave us presents, and showed us Polaroids
of their trip, our father sniffed, smiled,
and winked: his two boys no longer virgins.

Bringing Home the Bacon

Sharron Hough

Nothing is as tasty
As a pinky fatty strip
Of crispy ribbon bacon
And its salty oily drip
It goes back as far as fairytales
Stories read to soothe
And conjures dreams of pleasure
Of bacon—greasy smooth
It was no coincidence
Wolfie wanted pigs
The one he wanted most of all
Built his house of twigs
Cos everyone loves bacon
But more so if it's smoky
That piggy's choice of timber
Made it nice and oaky
Then piggy went to market
He did not return
But brekky rolls were sold that day
When will those piggies learn?

Piggy in the middle
Of a roasting spit
Bacon over open flame
Is always such a hit
Wrap a pig in blankets
Of bacon yes indeed
Cos bacon equals comfort
Of which we've all agreed
So, bring home the bacon
It's food of childhood tales
Three little pigs, their sticky ribs
And crispy little tails

The Birthday Boy's Bacon

Mark Hudson

I was hanging out with my friend Chris today,
and he is Irish, and he was born on St. Patrick's Day,
which is two days away.

Every Sunday, we usually go to a coffee
shop in Winnetka to drink coffee and draw with
our other friend Ryan, and beforehand we stop
at the exact same restaurant blocks away.

He ordered a different sandwich than usual.
It was a bacon sandwich, and the bacon was made
from duck. I don't know what the significance
of the duck was, but maybe they are running
out of pigs, and trying to get rid of ducks!

He gave me a sample of the bacon. It
was delicious. I had just ordered a measly
side—dish of tater tots.

We conversed over food. We ended up
talking about art, and the censorship of art.
Chris talked about the late mayor of Chicago
Harold Washington, and how back in the day
someone did a painting of Harold Washington
in women's clothing, and it was hanging in
the Art Institute and the government made
them take it down.

I told Chris I once wrote an eight–line
rhyming poem about Harold Washington,
something like, "Harold ate at Harold's
chicken shack, Harold had a heart attack,"
(Harold's Chicken Shack is a Chicago
chicken chain. I think Harold Washington
did die of a heart attack, he loved to eat.
One conspiracy–theorist spread rumors
he was assassinated.)

We discussed whether Harold's
Chicken was still around, and how
it used to be by Columbia College
in Chicago where we both studied.
Then for his birthday, I bought him
a coffee.

Tuesday is St. Patrick's Day.
Should I get some green bacon?

Breakfast All Day

Steven Deutsch

When I was eight
I was finally allowed
to go the four blocks
to Ernies
for breakfast out
with Joel and Marvin.
It was as grown up
as I have ever felt.

I had a bacon
and cheese omelette
and a plate of home fries
I could barely see over.
Who knew from bacon?
Who knew from an omelette?
My mom was not an adventurous cook
I breakfasted on Wheaties,
half a browning banana,
and an occasional bagel.

Over the years Ernies
became my home
away from home.

They did a BLT
so loaded with bacon
you had to pound it
with your palm
to get your mouth around it.
It's the place we ate
after my high school graduation,
and you could tell if a date
was worth your time
by her reaction to two eggs
sunnyside up
with extra bacon
and a toasted english.

They went under this year,
fast—fooded out
by MceeDees and Burger King
where there isn't much difference
between the breakfast sandwich
and its styrofoam box.

I walk by Ernies everyday.
I always stop for a minute—
not just
to relive
the fine memories
but because that corner
will always
smell of bacon.

A Sonnet to Bacon

Winston Plowes

Shimmering back bacon, a treasure–trove find
Royal rashers glisten, in hues of green and gold
White fat ermine trimmed in the lines of rind
Cut from metallic muscle meat tied and tightly rolled

Raw oil slick miracle with irresistible appeal
The Northern Lights in loin have commandeered my gaze
Lean sheen transparencies on the Silver slicers steel
Then to the slab the shining flesh, held high with mirror glaze

Carried forth with ceremony to the window on display
From pig to pan this miracle of colours all combine
In a lustrous pearl kaleidoscope of patterns all at play
Translucent tender succulence released from butchers twine

How did these wondrous colours infuse my breakfast treat?
Am I imagining all of this, or is it really in the meat?

Makin' the Bacon

Remngton Murphy

"Lay it on me," he smiled,
Pouring on his Old Spice aftershave charm,

"Give me some of those sizzling,
Dripping, greasy strips of goodness."

She frowned.
No surprise in that.

She hated being merely his laundress,
Belly warmer, short order cook.

Okay, he thought,
Suddenly turning sour,

If that's the way you want to have it,
Two can play that game.

"You know the way I like 'em,"
He blustered, "Extra crispy!"

And then, doubling down,
"Put on that apron, honey,

Let's hear some noise
With the pots and pans.

You know the way I like my little piggy,
Makin' the bacon!"

She disappeared in a hurry.
Meanwhile, he grinned contentedly,

Hardly able to believe
He could be so witty,

Because he, the upright Christian husband,
Had zealously, cleverly

Laid down the law.
After two shakes of a lamb's tail

She returned with his orange juice,
Sugar, cream, and coffee

Balanced on a plastic
Walt Disney dollar store platter

(Depicting Mickey and Minnie
Walking the dog,

Which happened to be Pluto).
"Here's your bacon," she said,

Begrudging her thinnest
Of Dalai Lama smiles,

As she noisily plunked down
A steaming bowl of oatmeal.

Oh, the outrage!
"What's this?" he thundered.

"I ask for bacon
And you give me this?

And please, I don't want to hear it,
Don't you dare say a word

About my blood pressure,
My diabetes, or my high cholesterol.

I do not have high blood pressure!"
With his face turning red,

Without batting an eye, she said,
"You're welcome."

Untitled Haiku

Mark Heatchote

rashers of bacon
sun has made an omelette
autumnal breakfast

Mmmm Bacon

An acrostic poem

Steven Borg

Mental benders all-nighters
Manifest cure for the Freedom Fighters
Mined hope from two words to rouse the dead alive to waken
Mmmm, Bacon!

Best cure for a hang-over!
Any time and any day of the week
Cadavers of swine fresh in the sizzling
Odours resurrecting the weak;
Nuff for a Vegan's game-over.

I blame my fierce love of bacon on my fifth great grandfather Joab Squire

Jennifer Clark

Some followed
the beaten path of buffalo
to discover salt springs.

Some, like Joab,
trekked great distances
to bring home bacon.

He once walked twelve miles,
shoulders sizzling
with twenty-five pounds
of bacon blazing his back.

As we drive along I—90,
plunging through summer's heat,
the past shimmers,

I see him through the haze,
lugging 200 pounds of maple sugar
from Huron to Sandusky.

Today the path is asphalt.

We reach North Carolina
and run into the ocean,
but not before my brother
lays a slender slice of bacon
across my coffee cup.

We hang our suits on the line
to dry and my brother starts dinner.
Joab still slogs along. It will take him
three days to return with two barrels of salt.

It's shrimp and scallops tonight.
I care for neither.
Just try it, my sister says.
I've sprinkled it with pancetta.
Italian bacon, you know. You'll love it.

O, salted meat!

The Pig's Wife at Forty

Laurie Byro

Our brick house needs repointing. North
winds blow through cracks and furrows.
Muddy paw prints smear the window glass;
drool forms rivulets on dusty door frames.

The flower beds outside the porch are trampled
beneath all the waxing and waning. Another wolf
is huffing at the door. Romance can be a messy
enterprise. We boiled the last one in a black kettle

that hung in the fireplace. Two spring clean-ups,
you could still smell scorched wolf-fur
on the gingham curtains I had hemmed. Behind
our house are tell-tale signs an interloper is back.

We have found pieces of egg and bloody feathers
from newly hatched swans. Once, I found
a downy stem without its petal-soft head. Lately,
after I curl behind my husband's rump, I root under

the covers for a plump red apple. I hear
jealous howling from the direction of the forest.
He keens like they all have done, wants
another taste of my tender flesh. Admittedly,

I let the wolf in while my husband was out making
our fortune. He chased me for a while, I could tell
by his mournful gold eyes it was inevitable what
would happen next. If I wanted a romp, he would

be the one—his sleek silver body, his skillful mouth.
But I am older, wiser to the ways of wolves.
I have read enough fairy tales to know, not all
end happily despite their promises. We got

dirty like he predicted. I luxuriated in a filthy froth.
But, in the end, he wanted to turn me into a silk
purse. He wanted to gobble me up. Turn me into
bacon. Not by the hair on my chinny—chin—chin.

Rent Party

Alan Walowitz

Moses came down from the mountain,
plenty tired and more than a little singed
from the nearness of the flame and, let's face it,
wandering through the desert is no picnic,
despite the occasional, and incidental, shrubbery.
The hungry folks who'd dragged their feet till now,
kvetchy, out–of–sorts, weary of promises—
no milk and honey far as they could see—
and when he arrived, he expected a welcome?
Man, what'd you expect while you were gone so long?
Who wouldn't have worshipped the golden onion,
or at least danced around its root, if only for dreams
of some yet–to–be fried potatoes.

He was finally spotted out the corner of one reveler's eye,
but no one shouted from joy, *Hey, Moses is back!*
He muttered to himself something like: *We are things of dry hours*
and the involuntary plan—and knew this
would not gonna be an easy sell,
especially for a guy slow of speech
who dropped into this rent party—while not totally uninvited—
with not much of a plan—
everybody knowing of his checkered past,
and, let's face it, no track record for bringing home the bacon.
And what was this he was carrying in his arms?
More unpaid labor nobody was exactly praying for.

drive by

Lucy Tyrrell

he likes to lie on the mound in his pen,
a smile curving on his bristly snout

tucked away in the woods by the road,
welded—wire fence, a shelter, a pile of straw

every day I drive by, I glance over,
peer in the pen, learn something more of his habits

if it is raining, he takes cover
under the small slanted roof

I never hear a sound, even if I lower
the window, call out piggy greetings

I never find him eating, or being fed,
he seems content, luxuriating on straw

his bulk enormous with folded pink ears,
skin rough between flakes of mud

one day,
the pen door
hangs wide open

I ache
for his sentience
smoked in strips

Tyson Foods Warns of Meat Shortage

Jan Chronister

and the nation panics—
OMG! What will we do without meat?

Don't ask me. I've done
fine since I last boiled
hot dogs in college
fifty years ago. Never
cooked a turkey
roasted a ham
flipped burgers
fried bacon.

Our house is not
a holiday destination—
no Christmas feasts
backyard cookouts
potluck favorites.

Guess we're prepared
for at least one pandemic
byproduct.

Centuries of Bacon

D. A. Bailey

Bringing home the bacon,
We've been doing it for centuries;
Dates to 1500 BCE,
When Romans called bacon *petaso,*
The "back" of a pig.

The first bacon factory,
Opened in 1770
By businessman John Harris,
Developed a special brining solution,
Called the "Wiltshire Cure" method.

Bacon was used to make explosives,
During World War II;
Donated leftover bacon grease,
Rendered fats created glycerine,
Created bombs, gunpowder, munitions.

In the Church of Bacon,
There are more than 25,000 members,
Who are commanded to "Praise Bacon";
All bacon praise is welcomed,
Love that sweeter, less salty taste.

Salad Days

Gerard Sarnat

Shiftless, heads down, drifting in one by one
from beat—up Chevies, Caddy LaSalles, Ford trucks,
some with walkers, wheelchairs, canes

they gather at Ruby's Diner,
the daring on treacherous high round blue soda fountain stools,
the rest behind bright red vinyl booths and white Formica tables.

Complaining Yesterday was better, once young men come
like clockwork for Sunday morning pork sausage and waffle brunch
— but mainly to nostalg buddies, chat up and waitress ogle

lecherous over dogs and malts, under '40s Technicolor® posters
of jitterbuggy Hayworthian women or Hellcat bomber plane models,
chattering away to the quarter jukebox tunes of their choosing,

Sentimental Journey, Shine On Harvest Moon,
You're Nobody 'Til Somebody Loves You,
anything by Crosby, Peggy, or Sinatra.

Decades past their prime, I assume mostly widowed or nevered,
these antiques reassemble from a bygone era,
yearn to be more than artifacts and regrets not on today's menu.

So once a month they meet to shun these grayer greener times'
unhappy healthy servings of 40% less fat fries, veggie delights,
and Cobbs — Honey, double us up on the bacon and vinaigrette.

The Ring

Colleen Moyne

It had been a year
Since the marriage ended
Broken fences were mended
and both had moved on

But the damned ring
still on her finger
seemed to represent
a troublesome loose end

Svelte and slim
when he'd first slipped it on
Those days were long gone
and chubbiness had set in

That ring stayed put
despite efforts to wrench and twist
it continued to resist
and maintain its hold

But now there was new love
and a new hand to hold
That stubborn piece of gold
just had to go

And wouldn't you know?
It came to them one morning
over a romantic breakfast
of rashers and eggs

They scooped up the dregs
of beautiful bacon fat
applied a generous slathering,
a little tug

and – just like that –
the ring slipped off
and clattered to the floor,
a troublesome loose end no more

My Secret Mistress

Helen M. Asteris

Sizzle low and whisper to me, sweet slut of the culinary world,
You curvy streak of pink ruin
Allow me to fold you into a yeasty caress
and take you wholly and deeply into me,
Devour you in your entirety and then, like the pig I am,
Turn to your bronzed and bubbling sister and savour her too.

Olfactory temptress, be you my morning glory
or night time naughtiness,
You draw me again and again to your frigid den of desire,
to feast at every hour,
Tearing at the constraints that bind until I can lay my hands
upon your delicious density
I toss you wantonly to the flames, and watch
as you shiver in ecstasy,
Hissing and spitting like the beast you are.

An allure so strong, you tease and torment my every sense,
Taunting even the most determined herbivore
To twist and writhe and ultimately contrive,
To break bonds and promises writ deep and held true,
All cast aside for a taste of the forbidden flesh.

Oh deep mystique of smoke and flame,
When alcoholic demons hang heavy from evenings past,
There is no cure but you. Wrapped in a slice of soft white,
Buttered, basted in sauce and served with tea.
Dear bacon, unholy addiction, my secret mistress.

Makin' Bacon

Martin Shaw

Bolt
through the brain, ascending worth.
No Country for Old Men.
Soul is leaking
to a soakaway.
Black pudding.

The Isle of Meat.
Supermarket logistics.
Oxymoron.

'Fava beans
and a nice chianti.
You fly back to school now
little Starling.'

Cushioned on a bandage
in a polystyrene tray,
a belly wound.
Pork
is uncomfortably blushing,
a riper shade of entrails.

The Real Culture War

Sy Brand

Starbucks is bleeding.

Salted warcries pounding drums
against the cloy of autumn, cloven
hooves severed from cured
belly and arrowshot
over sticky table thick with
sickly cart—ride squash oozing
from split bulbous flesh
when all they wanted
was a coffee break.

The only difference
in obsession
between pumpkin spiced lattes
and bacon
is misogyny.

Charmer

Holly McCann

He said
"I love you like I love bacon",
And I was supposed to be flattered.
Why would I want
To be consumed so ravenously,
Held on a pedestal,
Used as a bargaining chip?
But then he told me
"For the longest time,
I avoided bacon because I thought it was bad for me.
Now I know better
And I love you like something I went too long without."
Yeah, maybe my heart melted a little.
The charmer.

Better Than a B.L.T.

John Bost

Bacon, lettuce, and tomato?
Ham and Swiss on multigrain
With some lettuce and tomato –
But, forget the mayo. Just plain
Ham and Swiss on multigrain.
Yes, just for now it will sustain.
And could you wrap it up to go?
Ham and Swiss on multigrain
With some lettuce and tomato.

Beware of Bacon

Debbie Wiess

The Earth—shattering news was
announced. The World Health
Organization in a startling public
revelation officially declared that
beloved bacon had been found
to be a proven carcinogen.
The evidence was irrefutable.
The conclusion devastating.
Bacon, the scientists said, should
be avoided like the plague.
So avert your eyes if you can
to avoid enticement when passing
the product in the supermarket aisle.
And stop up your ears so you
cannot hear the beckoning of its
deadly siren's song.

But oh! to think how when grilled
on a skillet the striated grey, white
and pink strips bubble and sizzle!
The scent most alluring wafting
from the stovetop and filling nasal
passages with its promise of warm
crispy smoky deliciousness.
The very thought invoking feelings
the most rhapsodic. Nonetheless,
one must not forget how imperatively
it is recommended to avoid this
processed meat though it be such a
favorite treat. Whether for breakfast
or adding a dash of flavor to any repast.
Mastering such temptation is difficult.
And resistance in the end is futile.
So invariably and inevitably a new
package somehow miraculously
ends up in one's shopping cart.

Bringing it Home to South Australia

Alex Robertson

The Continent responsible for boars
Western Europe in particular
Germany, the UK and France
Providing pork to the free settlers
In various forms and ways

A cut unlike any other
Traditionally,
      utilising everything but the squeal
Barossa paddocks known for vines
Rather than piggeries
Deutsch traditions
      spreading to the Adelaide Plains
Found in Barossa Fine Foods and Wintulichs
Trading on Bavarian and Austrian ancestors
And the towns Gawler and Nuriootpa

A close relation to German pressed protein
Fritz: a minced cold sausage
          called Devon or Polony elsewhere
This luncheon meat
          (related to its cousin Spam)
Declares one's Britishness
In the post—War era
For cucumber in one's sandwiches
Is not the only option
For an afternoon 'delicacy'

Frenchman Nicolas Baudin's decision
Delivered in times of exploration
Guilty of introducing feral species
For breeding and later consumption
A porcine food source in the Antipodes
No tyranny of culls or baiting
The free—range type wiped out with fire
          in this Millennium's early years
Strong winds the culprit
The swine unable to escape in Flinders Chase
Their ancestors transported to the Island
Some 200 years ago…

European delicacies brought across the Equator
A bit of boar in Wakefield's plan
Below Goyder's Line…
Not just bacon
          but the whole hog

Prose

Prose

Brown or red?

Christopher Tattersall

He daydreamed of breakfast. Work was stressful and his only solace was the thought of baked beans, hash browns, bacon and of course sauce but which one? There was always a debate over the variety of sauce – red tomato ketchup or fruity brown?

Brown or red? The decision was complex, it always had been and always would be.

Sausages, he would have sausages, two of them to match the number of bacon rashers.

Brown or red? The verdict was weighing heavily on him.

Would he have mushrooms if they were on offer? Of course not. He smiled to himself as he remembered his Corporal telling him how mushrooms were first discovered – by a demon cleaning the fungus between the third and fourth toes of the devil.

Brown or red? He had to decide soon, very soon. It was almost time.

Eggs! He had forgotten about eggs, now there was a hard decision – scrambled, fried or poached? The decision to have scrambled eggs was tough, but easy compared to whether it would be brown or red.

What about a vegetarian breakfast? That was an easy decision – no. The brown or red conundrum remained.

Hungry from nerves or simply through a lack of food he wasn't sure. He knelt carefully in his bulky protective clothing and paused to regulate his breathing. A bead of sweat dripped from his forehead on to the inside of his visor, slightly obscuring his view of the improvised device in front of him. Again he imagined the breakfast he had planned for himself back at barracks if everything went his way.

For the last time he considered his options. Brown or red?

He cut the red wire.

Diary

Wayne Scheer

I woke this morning thinking about the best way to kill myself.

Maybe it's the weather. The sky looks dead−cat gray.

I really shouldn't be depressed. I have a good job, plenty of money, a girlfriend, food in my refrigerator and an apartment that costs way too much but keeps rain from dripping on my head.

I should wake happy, maybe bop the baloney after a sexy dream. Then I should shower, eat a couple of eggs and call Ella to see if she wants to do something tonight.

I even work from home so I wake when my eyes open and not when the alarm clock rattles me out of bed.

I'm 24 years old and I design computer games. How cool is that?

And yet the clouds outside my window look like a death shroud and I'm wondering if shooting myself is the way to go.

(Way to go. Get it? I'm a regular Louis C.K.)

Ella and I had a good meal at a nice restaurant last night. Afterward, she came back to my place. We watched a little TV and I showed her a new project I've been working on. She's not really into gaming so I didn't get too technical. Then we fucked. The next morning she got up before me and made breakfast – French toast and bacon.

It doesn't get any more normal than that. But I must have had that dream again because I woke thinking when I put the gun in my mouth, I should angle it up for maximum effect.

I didn't get much sleep last night because of the storm. It sounded like the neighborhood was under attack, thunder bombed. I don't know why, but it got me thinking about hell and heaven. In hell, you do the same thing, over and over, without emotion. In heaven, you do something you love until you stop loving it. Then you do something else you love, until you don't. Which got me wondering if I'm living in heaven or hell?

I called Ella to share my epiphany. She said there was still some bacon left in my fridge. "Fry two strips and call me later in the morning."

She was right. A good bacon and egg breakfast and my suicide thoughts dissipated like any other dream. But I'm left wondering if my life is too easy. At 24, maybe I'm not ready to settle into an easy life.

But I love what I do for a living and I love Ella, although I've never told her. I don't want to give up my job and I can't imagine life without Ella.

I call her, but all I get is her answering machine. I thank her for the bacon advice and say I'll call back later.

My Least Favorite Things

Mir—Yashar Seyedbagheri

My older sister Nancy and I list our least favorite things nightly.

For Nancy, it's *The Sound of Music*, Republicans, starched smiles, and proclamations of parental love. She says love's contrived, rife with false promises. People always leave. They never really love you.

I can't argue with that.

For me, my least favorite things are bacon without fat, the sound of bacon sizzling, drunk fathers, football players, beer, war, trains, wanderlust, and parental love.

We relish firing fusillades at the world. But some nights, we try to think of our favorite things. Just in case luck decides to visit us, Nancy says.

But we can't conjure any favorites. We search the night sky, the moon, even watch *The Addams Family*. The moon inevitably leaves. *The Addams Family* is full of quirky kindness.

We prefer hating. It's easy.

The Diet

Niles Reddick

On New Year's Eve, I was short of breath because I bent over to tie my shoes because I had to make a grocery store run for black—eyed peas, ham, and cornbread mix. My noticeable belly pushed all the internal organs around, constricting my diaphragm. I knew how I had come to be this way—the belly, the enlarged breasts that needed a bra not made for men, and the swollen foot pushing tiny bones. When I got to the grocery, I pushed the cart, rollicking down the aisles in search of the New Year's Day meal.

On New Year's Day, I ate the black—eyed peas my wife had cooked in broth with bacon, and the ham, but I avoided the cornbread. When the key lime pie came out of the box and was cut, I waved off the offer. I never said a word about going on a diet. That night, I dreamed someone was baking bread, the smell permeated the house, and it smelled better than an orgasm felt. When I awoke to the sound of noises, I thought it was thundering, and I learned it was my belly noises. I had eggs, bacon, coffee, and my belly continued to rumble. At a stoplight on the way to work, I glanced over and saw a fat guy eating a donut and wanted to run him off the road, steal his donut. When I got to my office, I had to wipe the saliva drooling on my chin. When everyone at the office talked about the sugar—free shortbread cookies in the break room and how healthy they were, I cooked my lunch bacon in the microwave, went back to my cube and faked work.

A month later, forty pounds of fat were gone. I'm sure there's another American who found them because of the law of conservation of mass. I've been rearranged, but that fat has latched onto someone else, and I continue to shrink. One pound yesterday, two today. People at the office are whispering about stage four cancer, and I probably look like another cancer statistic. I'll buy some more clothes when we get paid in a couple of weeks, but I can barely hold my breeches up. A supervisor told me, "You think you're still a teenager? Pull up them pants."

When I see myself in the mirror before a shower, I think I need to tighten the sagging skin. I can't get it sucked and tucked like famous people. I don't make that much money, but I resolve I'll walk it off—before work, during lunch, and at night. I think I'll have to do sit–ups to tighten the belly sag, and I'll have to do push–ups to bring muscle back and sculpt arm flab. It's not easy, but I should look good enough to bury soon. I owe it all to bacon and eggs. I also owe a case of gout in my right big toe to bacon and hope I can find a purine–free bacon product I can substitute.

People Are Idiot's

Tom Hazuka

Morgan stares at the Facebook page, left hand fingers drumming on his thigh. Doing nothing is one option, and possibly the best one. Anyone can make an inadvertent error. But this doesn't feel inadvertent. This feels smug and stupid, and if it doesn't exactly break Morgan's heart, it does trample hopes he has dared to let build for the last three weeks and five days.

If a relationship can't survive a couple being Facebook friends, then it's hopeless, right? Face facts and move on. But Morgan likes Vanessa, a lot, as in he might actually love her, and for reasons far beyond physical attraction—though the sex is the best he's ever known, hands down and everywhere else hands can end up.

But "People are idiot's"? The screwed–up plural is one thing; chances are he has done worse, without noticing (because if he'd noticed he would have fixed it). It's the comment itself that troubles him more, a response to a post supporting universal background checks for gun buyers. Morgan searches for ambiguity, but it's hard to conclude otherwise than that Vanessa's "idiot's" are people like him, the 90% (he googled it) of Americans who want universal background checks.

Who could be against keeping potentially dangerous people from getting firearms? Even most NRA members support background checks. How is it possibly an idiotic idea? Morgan considers adding a comment to the thread, but words fail him, and so does courage. Besides, he knows it's an exercise in futility. Most people's minds are made up.

His isn't.

He closes his eyes as a memory ten years old pops into view: day one of his freshman comp class at a huge state university, taught by a surprisingly hot graduate student. Morgan congratulated himself on his luck as she went over the syllabus. Then, on the middle of page two, she reached her "Plajerism" policy.

He figured she'd blush at her mistake and make some witty remark that would cement his crush on her. But she just read the section and moved on to her attendance policy.

There was no way in hell he'd say anything in class, but Morgan debated going up to her afterward. He even took a few steps toward the lectern where she stood, but half a dozen students already hovered around her. He wondered if one of them would mention the error. He wondered if anyone else in the class even *knew* it was an error.

Morgan left without a word. He never did tell her. In the end he had to admit she made him a better writer—though it rankled when he got a B from someone who couldn't spell "plagiarism." For the record, she also said "like" too often.

Five weeks since their first date, and until three minutes ago Morgan had marveled at how he and Vanessa liked the same things. *Citizen Kane* and *Plan 9 from Outer Space. The Great Gatsby* and gin gimlets. Tofu burritos and veggie burgers perversely topped with bacon. Staying in bed till noon on Sundays, but hardly sleeping after waking at nine.

Politics? He can't remember if they've discussed politics, which seems semi—impossible now that he thinks about it. That stuff always comes up, right? Unless it doesn't. Unless there are so many better things to talk about.

One topic that had come up was *30 Rock*. They both loved the show. Morgan takes heart. If Vanessa were channeling Ann Coulter she couldn't stand Alec Baldwin, right? She had especially liked the "Dealbreakers" episode, to the point of quoting some of Tina Fey's lines, and Morgan had cracked up.

Now he's starting to feel the other meaning of "crack up." Morgan knows that's melodramatic; he's not losing his mind, just the sense of rightness with the world he has felt since his first five minutes with Vanessa. He has never clicked so completely with a woman before. His four years with Ginny after college never felt like more than good fun, and when the fun faded it was a fairly easy kiss goodbye for both of them. So much more is at stake now, despite their short time together.

Gnawing his lip, more nervous than before their first date, he types, "Idiots are people too." He stares at the words for nearly a minute before deleting them. He substitutes, "Some of my best friends are idiots," and adds a smiley–face emoji.

Feeling like a moron, and like he has no choice, Morgan hits the return key.

Substitutions

Jill Olson

I have always been a proponent of purity.

I have never, nor will I ever, accept substitutions.

I am puzzled when something tries to be what it is not.

I am frustrated when something has a name which turns out to be an inaccurate moniker.

I am angered when something makes promises, then doesn't deliver.

Therefore, I will NEVER accept turkey bacon.

Bacon Pig

Chuka Susan Chesney

All we have left in the way of meat are two hot dogs and bacon. We started staying inside a week ago and have already run out of chicken and ground turkey. Our Maine Coon eyes the butter. He's prancing around the table, watching us build open–faced sandwiches out of sliced hot dogs, strips of bacon, mustard, diced onion, lettuce, and toast. Normally I crumble my bacon into pieces and set them in front of Biggie Pig's nose on the empty placemat next to mine.

But I find myself thinking, maybe I should eat this. Maybe I won't have any meat later. I toss Biggie a tiny bit of bacon. His massive ruff rises as he smells one of his favorite snacks and dots his nose around the quilted fabric, trying to locate the luscious morsel. He teethes the bacon and shakes it, as if to break its neck. Then he blinks his eyes at me, wanting another piece. My husband Drew takes pity on him and creates a pyramid of tidbits.

Well, I guess as soon as the bacon's gone, we could eat some frozen dinners from Trader Joe's. Stir–fried rice with scrambled eggs. Kung Pao Chicken. Or we could make omelettes. We have eggs and mushrooms.

Our son calls, wanting to know if we need anything in this new situation we've never experienced. It's raining outside. The sky is gray and chilly for Southern California. There's hardly any traffic noise — you can hear doves tweeting in the ficus. I've never seen Catalina Island look so clear in our view. It's steeper than I thought it was.

"Mom, do you have enough food?" asks James' voice on my cell. He's never asked me that. No one has ever asked me if I had enough food.

"Yes, but we're almost out of meat. All we have left now is bacon," I reply. James knows I don't care much for bacon.

"Mom, I'm going to drive around and look for some meat," he insists.

"Where? The shelves at the stores are empty, aren't they?"

"I know where to go," he tells me.

An hour later I hear his car in the driveway. I open the bathroom window, and start to sing "Figaro" through the screen. I want to be like one of those Italian neighbors singing to each other on their balconies above the dark streets of the virus.

"Look, Mom, I got you some frozen burgers and chicken! I went to a barrio store in my neighborhood. The suburbanites haven't cleaned out their shelves yet!" James holds up a bag, filled with bulgy packages, then leaves it out on the porch. I tell him thank you and start crying. He drives away. I don't know when I'll see him again.

Drew and I work up the courage to put on gloves and bring the bag to the garage. We set the meat on a work table. Drew pulls out a package of six ground beef patties and squirts the front of it with rubbing alcohol. The plastic starts to melt. Next there is a huge package of chicken.

"I guess I won't spray this," he says, and rubs the plastic with a Chlorox Wipe.

We stash the hamburgers in the freezer for next week and

the chicken in the meat drawer.

Next day, we're sitting at the table eating roasted chicken. Biggie leaps on the table and strides near our plates, his massive tail trailing like a bush behind him. We put some of the gristle on his placemat. There's plenty of chicken, so I tear pieces into a stack. Biggie shakes his mane and purrs while he chews the meat.

This morning someone told us in an email our city's Fire Department will bring seniors food from the market — even those who are only in their early 60s. We can call and tell them what we want. James leaves a bag of kibble on our patio while we're out for a stroll. Hopefully there will be enough meat.

Call of the Wild

Allan J. Wills

Texas Tech University.
"Pig pheromone proves useful in curtailing
bad behavior in dogs."
ScienceDaily, 24 August 2014.

"Hey! Rider needed here."

"Where to?" The front Eats rider on the rank stepped forward pushing his grid.

"Old Mrs Thompson second floor on Main and Hay ordered this."

"Fuck! She's got a couple of beagles that always rush out and go for ya nuts."

"You need this stuff," the second up rider offered.

"What is it?" Front rider took the proffered small aerosol.

"Wild Boar essence. Spray a bit on yourself and no dog will touch you." The second rider's face was deadpan.

"Are ya shitting me? How do ya know it works?"

"My Grandpappy was a postie in the old days. On Tuesdays and Thursdays Gran made him bacon sandwiches for breakfast. Took him a while to work out why the dogs never barked at him on those days."

The first rider packed his hot pack then sprayed some of the potion on his chest and legs. A faintly rancid, slightly wild and gamey perfume wafted over the group of delivery riders, mingling with their own sweaty odours.

The electric bike whirred around the corner onto Main. Halfway towards Hay a stray mongrel caught a whiff of the scent and gangled out of a side alley in pursuit of the source. A little further on, a man walking a crossbreed terrier lost control of his charge as the terrier slipped his collar and belted after the mongrel.

Mrs Thompson opened the door to the Eats rider. The mongrel and the terrier reached the second—floor landing just as the beagles pushed forward from behind Mrs Thompson's legs.

The four dogs looked at each other, hackles up and sniffing, and then at the Eats rider, before fixing on the box of food in the rider's hands above them.

Leaping and plunging the dogs tore the box to shreds, snarling and growling as they devoured the pork belly and rice.

Needing Bacon

Ruth Z. Deming

My first cuppa tea for the day. Ah, I drank from a teacup I bought at Mr Joe's Concession Shop. Everything was second—hand.

Warming my hands on the gorgeous blood—red cup, I reached in the fridge to make my breakfast.

Whole—wheat bread, I popped into the toaster—oven. Philadelphia Cream Cheese I put on my small Ikea table, and the bacon.

Where was the bacon?

I searched in all the spill—proof drawers, and even in the huge freezer. Why would anyone freeze bacon?

Good Lord.

I removed the toast from the toaster—oven and wearing a jacket and hood, ran across the street to my neighbor Nancy's.

Her little white dog began barking as if I were gonna rob the house. Nancy peeked out.

"Can I borrow two slices of bacon?" I asked.

"We don't eat it," she said.

"Why not?" I asked.

"It's not healthy," she said.

I ran back across the street, raindrops soaking my blue sweat shirt.

I turned the toaster—oven back on, spread the toast with cream cheese, cut up a red tomato, and ate the most delicious breakfast sandwich ever.

Sans bacon.

Norma and the Kid from Tallahatchie

Tobi Alfier

Norma had been running the farm herself ever since she chased off her cheating liar of a husband, divorce papers exchanged in the mail. She had the muscles to lift hay bales into the back of the Jeep the same as any man could do—seven of them fit. She knew all about lambing, and when to call the vet. She knew all about planting and going to market with plants and animals alike. She got along just fine.

But anger only carries a woman so far, so when Norma met the kid from Tallahatchie when he slipped onto the bar stool next to hers one Friday night, it was written in the stars. The twelve–year age difference was a small issue indeed—Norma being a woman who took good care of herself and had farming muscles to boot. The kid had his choice of sitting anywhere, and he chose next to her.

How to keep him in her house and in her bed? Dangling a tractor in front of him was gonna keep him for just a second. Norma had to cook. And cook she would. As soon as he got a taste of her wicked–ass chicory coffee and her specialty, biscuits and gravy Benedict, he'd be hers for as long as she wanted. And as she watched him sleeping that night, the first time anyone had put a dent in that pillow in ages, Norma knew she'd want it to be for a long time. She wanted him to look out the window with her and watch the wildflowers bloom, then put up the Christmas tree six months later. And she knew she'd want him to do it again and again.

Norma made her Benedict using bacon gravy instead of sausage. She cooked up a ton of bacon, crispy as if God reached down and borrowed fire from the devil, then chopped it nice and fine. Thrown into a white sauce with a sprinkle of cracked pepper, you could eat it right from the pot, but that wasn't good enough.

The biscuits smelled so good from the oven they woke him up. His name was Tim, she'd finally asked. Tim came downstairs and didn't even go outside to smoke, he just waited. Norma took those biscuits, draped gravy over, then crisp bacon slices crossed in an "X marks the spot" and a perfectly poached egg. Being the polite kid he was, Tim waited for her. Together they had breakfast and a little conversation plenty satisfying.

After a full day of farm chores they met up on the porch for spicy Bloody Marys, garnished with a beautiful stalk of celery from the garden, and a slice of bacon from the morning. All the lonelies gave way to a feeling of warmth and what was meant to be.

Bourbon brought them together, and bacon kept them together. Norma and Tim, the kid from Tallahatchie, crafting themselves a life and love no one had predicted and no one had ever thought possible.

All About Bacon

Julius De Smedt

I have never heard of bacon.

Well, that is not true. Although I never heard the word bacon, I did know about bacon.

It all started one rainy day. My best friend from the good old primary school days, Johnny, and I enjoyed a milkshake in a cosy restaurant. He loved the chocolate flavour. I preferred strawberry.

"I'm going to emigrate to England," he pronounced, spoiling the day.

"You can't," I screamed, devastated.

Everybody in the restaurant looked at us.

"Sorry, I did not mean to scream." Embarrassed, I looked down, folding my hands on my lap. Tears rolled down my cheeks.

Being kind, Johnny saved my bacon from the fire. That, just so you know, is a term I learned much later, and still do not know how to use correctly.

Johnny put his arm around my shoulders and said: "I will sponsor your air ticket as a birthday present, then you come and visit me. What do you say about that?"

I think there is a saying, 'half an egg and bacon is better than none'. Maybe that is a wrong direct translation. I accepted the invitation anyway.

Family and friends were excited for me, helping in any way they could to prepare me for the journey. They even assisted me at my attempt to learn English.

"When you greet someone," I was told, "you must say, 'Hey, I don't like you.' When you want to thank someone, you should say, 'You saved my bacon.'"

They gave me a few more tips which I practiced daily. I was excited to impress Johnny with my good knowledge of English.

When I arrived in England, I could not wait to see Johnny. He arrived early the next morning.

"Hey, Johnny, I don't like you!" I exclaimed.

Johnny smiled happily at me and greeted me the way we used to. He had no reason to impress me as I was impressed by him already.

"I have a little present in the car for you," he said.

"You already gave me a present by inviting me." I only said that so he would not think I was greedy.

Johnny laughed. "You must have something that will make you think of me daily. The trip will eventually be forgotten."

"I will never forget this trip," I argued, following Johnny.

At the car, Johnny gave me a puppy.

"O, cute," I said, pressing the puppy to my heart. Then I remembered to thank him.

I said: "You saved my bacon, Johnny. What will we call him?"

Johnny laughed. "What about calling him Bacon?"

We decided to do that after he explained to me how little I know about English.

The next morning, I woke up, hungry and ready for breakfast. I searched for Bacon without success.

With my heart beating like African drums I rushed towards the reception to enquire if someone saw Bacon.

But on my way I saw Bacon waiting for me in the dining room. His tail wagging at top speed, his tongue slapping wind.

"You silly thing," I exclaimed. "How dare you beat me to breakfast."

Being in England, I expected eggs and bacon for breakfast. I was disappointed to find ample egg, but no bacon.

I enjoyed the breakfast regardless of the lack of bacon.

The third day I woke up earlier than normal. Like the previous days, Bacon was already gone. And, as usual, I found him in the dining room. Only, this time I was a bit earlier. I caught Bacon having his breakfast.

"Bacon, you scoundrel," I scowled at him. "You are eating my bacon!"

Two days later I left England, bringing home my Bacon. A year later I gave Bacon some bacon for his birthday.

I still do not know English, but I have learned all about Bacon.

Porkies

Eileen O'Reilly

The supermarket delivers Janet's order on Friday; on Saturday, Harry loads up his bike panniers and delivers food to his elderly mother.

Since government guidelines allow one period of exercise a day, but counts checking up on a 'vulnerable person' as essential travel, Harry has the perfect excuse to get away from home for a few hours.

The initial novelty of self–isolation in those early months of 2020 soon wore thin. Janet decided the pandemic was the perfect excuse to begin a healthy eating regime, especially with some of their former 'essentials' in short supply.

'You're going to have a lot of time on your hands, Harry. Working from home is great, but if this goes on for much longer, that work is going to dry up and then what will you do?'

As Harry couldn't immediately come up with a satisfactory response, Janet continued.

'Don't think you're going to spend all your time lying on the sofa drinking beer and watching box–sets. We might not be able to go for drives in the country and lunch in a pub, but there are other things you can do.'

'Such as?'

'You're always saying you want to start a vegetable garden if only you had the time; well now you have. You can order seeds online. Just think of all those lovely veggies in a couple of months. Fresh salad; our own potatoes and tomatoes. A couple of chickens to provide eggs.'

Harry thought about it. It did sound like a good idea, and Janet was right, work was already beginning to tail off.

For a moment he had this picture in his head: Janet, slim and smiling, strolling around the garden wearing something floaty, a basket of freshly picked fruit and vegetables on her arm; himself stripped to the waist, bronzed muscles rippling in the sun as he dug the rich earth; Janet gazing at him, her eyes full of promise . . .

'Harry! You're not listening.'

'Sorry, love. What did you say?'

'I said, it will be good to stop eating processed food and to reduce our meat consumption. Good for us, and for the environment too. It will give us something positive to focus on to get us through and keep us healthy.'

'When you say "reduce", what do you mean?'

'Go vegetarian. Not straight away, obviously. We can't do that until the veggie garden is established. But we can work our way through what's currently in the freezer, and then just not replace it. I mean, who really knows what's in half the food we eat, or where it's come from?' Janet was on a roll.

'We'll eat what's fresh and in season. Buy from the farm shop or local butcher and know that they can trace the animal back to a specific farm. Eat less of it, but pay for good quality and savour it.'

Put like that, Janet did seem to have thought of everything. Then . . .

'All that extra exercise and healthy living will do your blood pressure no end of good. By the end of this crisis, you could be half the weight you are now. We'll start by cutting out salty bacon and sausages, and by grilling food instead of frying it.'

'No bacon? What about our Sunday breakfasts?'

'A bowl of porridge and some fruit is much healthier. It's a pity we can't persuade your mum to stop eating meat too.'

'She's seventy−eight, Jan. She's not going to change her habits now, and why should she?'

'You're right. She'll probably ask us to double her order, just to be contrary.'

The weeks pass. Harry cycles ten miles every morning, rain or shine − usually a couple of loops round the reservoir Mondays to Fridays, and up into the hills to his mother's remote cottage on Saturdays.

While he's out from under her feet, Janet does an hour's Pilates, checks what vegetables are ready for eating and looks up recipes online. Harry seems very appreciative of her cooking these days, eating everything on his plate and praising new dishes, even though some of them don't turn out quite as expected due to the difficulty in getting hold of the recommended spices.

As he pedals up the steep track to his childhood home, Harry marvels at how fit he has become in the months since he stopped sitting behind a desk and started getting out into the fresh air.

The vegetable garden has exceeded his expectations, providing almost all their daily needs and with some to spare. And who would have thought, on that first day when he finally dragged his bike from the shed and wobbled his way along the lane, that he'd soon be averaging fifty miles a week?

As well as his mother's shopping order, this morning he's brought runner beans, new potatoes, the first ripening tomatoes, some fresh eggs from their own chickens, and a small plastic container of strawberries.

His mother is sitting outside in the sun when he arrives. Mindful to stick to social distancing rules, Harry dismounts outside the gate and shouts a greeting. She seems cheerful enough, despite him being her only visitor. But Emily Watson has never needed the company of people, preferring birdsong to gossip, and spending her evenings listening to plays and concerts on the radio.

'I'll put your shopping in the box, Mum,' Harry shouts, opening the lid and removing a small package wrapped in tin–foil before transferring the contents of his panniers to the box. After a few more words of shouted conversation, Harry waves and sets off back down the track towards home.

His route takes him along a winding lane with a stream running beside it. There is a bench facing the water where he likes to sit for a while, and eat the crispy bacon roll his mum has prepared for him every Saturday morning since he explained Janet's healthy eating regime.

And what Janet doesn't know won't hurt her. Will it?

Suppertime

Carl 'Papa' Palmer

Standing in my kitchenette, pouring the can of Van Camp pinto beans into a saucepan, I picture the big stainless steel kettle Mom used for soups or stews, boiling canning jars, sterilizing baby bottles, and now, as I fix my meal, I'm reminded she also used it for soaking beans.

Mom had a bean formula:

1 lb. of dried beans = 2 cups
2 cups triple when cooked = 6 cups
6 cups = 8 servings

With six kids she'd usually start out with three or four pounds of dried beans.

"Nothing says you can't have leftovers."

Many mornings I'd see that kettle on the kitchen counter by the sink with floating milky husks and skins of submerged beans, soaking since before I got up. She made sure they stayed covered by an inch or so of water, never drained and rinsed like her rarely used red and white Betty Crocker cookbook advised.

"Why pour God's vitamins and minerals down the drain?"

She'd stir her beans occasionally, add more water and skim off the floaters until early afternoon. *"Time to start supper,"* putting the kettle on the stove while my sisters set the table for our later evening meal.

As I shake dried onion flakes to hydrate in my warming beans, I remember the tears stung from my eyes as Mom chopped onions fresh from the garden into her pot, green parts and all. She'd rub Morton salt on her hands, *"Gets the smell off my fingers."*

While biting open the cellophane and cutting chunks of smoked beef jerky into my beans for flavor, I remember when growing up, meat wasn't always there at our house. Saved bacon grease in a Crisco can or chicken broth made do when we didn't have that ham hock or soup bone she'd sometimes get from the butcher, no matter if it were beef or pork.

My store—bought pack of Sara Lee muffins is a poor replacement for the hot steaming aroma of browned yellow cornbread from Mom's black tin fresh out of the oven. My sister still makes hers that same way and tried to tell me how.

She even wrote it down:

1 cup sifted flour
1 cup of combined yellow and white cornmeal
4 teaspoons baking powder
1 teaspoon baking soda
½ teaspoon salt
1 cup buttermilk
2 eggs
½ cup of yesterday's bacon grease
¼ cup sugar
1 tablespoon sour cream
1 tablespoon apple cider vinegar

Put flour, sugar, baking powder, salt, baking soda, cornmeal in a bowl.

Add eggs, buttermilk, sour cream, vinegar and bacon grease

Use rotary hand mixer (never an electric mixer or blender), mix until almost smooth, not too much (like a bowl of oatmeal).

Pour into a buttered 9 x 9 x 2 inch pan.

Bake at 425 degrees for 25 minutes.

Carrying my meal, still in the saucepan to the foldout metal tray table by the couch, I think back to our family supper table...

We wait for Mom to take off her apron and sit at her end of the table. Dad sits on the other end, three boys on one side, three girls on the other. She ladles out eight bowls of steaming hot beans beside a 3 x 3 inch cornbread cake and a cold glass of fresh cow's milk.

Together we say grace while smiling at the feast in front of us.

With a chorus of *"Father, Son, Holy Ghost"* and a nod from Dad, we all dig in.

"Amen," I whisper to my quiet room and turn up the sound on the apartment TV.

Bacon for Eternity

Samuel Gulliksson

Bill was dead before the ambulance arrived. His body lay right next to the chair he had fallen from – the chair, at the head of the table, that had been his for the last 15 years.

The four plates of breakfast still stood on the table. Bill's plate was half full and the remaining bacon strips had already grown cold and stiff. The two plates on the left side of the table were almost spotless – like crocodiles, Donny and Harry had quickly devoured all their food and left the table before Bill collapsed. On the fourth plate, on the right side of the table, some orange wedges, lettuce and two slices of rye bread were neatly arranged. Completely untouched.

Waiting for the paramedics to drive from the next town over – at least a twenty–minute drive – Linda started cleaning. What else was there to do? She had already sent Donny and Harry upstairs to change clothes so they would look respectable when the paramedics would come to pick up Bill's body.

She gathered all the plates from the table and scraped the leftovers into the trash. She hated wasting food, but there was no time to eat now. And who would want to eat stale old bacon? No! Into the trash it went. Then rinse all the plates and stack them in the dishwasher. Maybe she should start it now so it would be done by the time they were back from the hospital?

Bill's insulin pen, which she had carefully placed next to his plate right before breakfast as she always did, also went into the trash. It wouldn't be needed any more. She wiped the table with the dishcloth and gathered all the crumbs in her left hand. She rinsed the dishcloth, hung it over the faucet to dry, wiped the sink with a paper towel to get rid of the remaining crumbs and then washed her hands. Order was restored. Except the dead body on the floor.

Linda hurried upstairs and put on a pair of black dress pants and a maroon long-sleeved knitted sweater. In the bathroom, she brushed her teeth and put on some mascara. While looking in the mirror she let out her hair and shook her head to get it to fall naturally. Yes, that's more appropriate.

When the doorbell rang, she was calm. On her way to open the door, she glanced around the house and smoothed her sweater over her breasts. Impeccable. Everything would be alright now.

Linda and Bill first met in high school and had been together ever since. The cherry trees were just about to blossom when Bill asked Linda to be his girlfriend. She thought the way he blew the hair out of his eyes was cute so she said yes. A whole life decided as easy as that.

Twelve years later, Harry was born. One year and four months after that, Danny was born. Two brothers, inseparable ever since. And Linda made sure they were loved. So did Bill. Just as Linda had planned.

Then came the house. And they finally had room for a big kitchen table where they could gather for breakfast and dinner. Linda made sure to spoil her family with all the food they wished for. Seeing their happy faces was what she lived for. But she wasn't sure, was it her or was it her food they loved most?

With time came the silence. The boys grew older, Bill grew rounder. Linda kept loving them. The house felt too big. Life was just a comfortable routine. Bill was promoted, their car grew bigger. Linda waved through the kitchen window when he left for work. The routine should have been a comfortable life. So why was it so hard to breathe?

The next morning Linda set out three plates. Maybe she should take the seat at the head of the table? No, it wasn't right – not yet. She opened the fridge and saw Bill's insulin on the top shelf. It was the only remaining trace of yesterday. When she was still someone's wife. She grabbed the cardboard boxes and emptied them in the trash can, covering the insulin pen from yesterday. No one would be able to tell the difference.

She returned to the fridge and took out a pack of bacon. With practiced movements she placed the thin slices of bacon in the cold frying pan and turned the heat to low. This was their favorite breakfast she had cooked almost every day for an eternity.

When the bacon was perfectly crispy, she removed it with the engraved kitchen tongs Bill gifted her on their anniversary this year. The inscription "For the love of my life... Bacon!" still wasn't funny, but it didn't hurt anymore. She cracked four eggs straight into the leftover bacon grease and then served them sunny–side up next to the bacon on two of the plates. For herself she cut half an orange, rinsed some lettuce and pulled two slices of rye bread from the bag. Just before calling Donny and Harry she took a deep breath and exhaled slowly. For the first time in years.

The Bust

J. D. Carter

"I'm telling you, he's up to something in that diner," Vera said. Her glossy heels clicked against the naked planks as she paced around the office of Orion Investigations. Her red dress twinkled like diamonds under a tide of blood. She took a long drag of a long cigarette and blew out a blue—grey plume.

Holden Porter sat at the desk watching her, listening to the click—clack of her steps. After some time, he said, "Take a seat, Mrs Phoenix, I'm sure I can help you."

"Well, you better. Because I know he's doing something. He's never home on time and there's these two horrible stinking whores in there all evening, flashing their eyes at him, pushing their tits together when he walks past," she said, scrunching her face in contempt. Then she slowly approached the desk, leaned over and said, "I need you to get him for me. Catch him in the act. I'll need proof. Photographs. Then I'll blackmail that deviant bastard for everything he's got." A devilish smile grew across her scarlet lips.

Holden stood, placed his brown fedora onto his head and rested his thumbs in his belt. "I'll take care of it, Mrs Phoenix. If that'll be all?"

Vera nodded, picked up her leather purse. "I'll be back in a couple of days with your payment," she said, and swayed her behind as she walked out of the office.

Holden poured two fingers of bourbon. He cradled the glass and looked out at the darkening sky over the city. Looks like rain tonight, he thought.

Jerry Phoenix owned Jerry's, a small diner at the end of Rosewood Avenue. Jerry was so lanky and lean he could be mistaken for otherworldly. His pale head was long and hairless, save for thin curved brows behind tortoise shell specs. He wore a white shirt buttoned to the jaw and long black pants that showed his socks when he walked.

Holden sat in his Buick Roadmaster parked in a snug alley. Under his fedora's brim he watched Jerry mill around in his diner behind tall dirt—flecked windows. He took orders, cleared tables and served the occasional omelet.

Holden picked up his coffee. A wisp of steam rose as he sipped. He flicked on the radio and harsh static filled the air. He fiddled with the knob. More static. Then he remembered the broken antenna. He flicked it off and the dial's orange glow faded.

Clouds cracked into heavy rain, drumming on the Buick's roof and sweeping through Rosewood Avenue in thick sheets. A red and blue neon above the diner's door fizzed and flickered.

Holden's eyes narrowed as a station wagon hissed through the rain and buckled onto the curb in front of Jerry's. A pale—faced woman with wiry black hair rushed out and scurried inside.

Close to midnight, a woman and one tall hairless man exited the diner and clambered into the station wagon.

The wagon's headlights sputtered through the rain as the engine started. Holden twisted the key. The Roadmaster growled into life, crawled out of the alley and sped off in pursuit.

He kept two cars distance behind them. Streetlights flashed across the bodywork as he rolled through the sodden streets. At a set of lights, he cracked the window, ushering in the scent of wet concrete. He lit a cigarette. Ribbons of smoke curled through the window.

Holden tailed them to a derelict warehouse. He parked the Buick and stepped out onto the wet flagstones, tucked his camera inside his beige trench coat and paced towards the warehouse.

Bars of moonlight from broken roof tiles offered a little light. Crumbs of glass crunched underfoot as he followed the muffled sounds of moaning and giggling and sharp slaps that cut through the gloom.

At the far side of the warehouse stood a small office. Holden leaned closer to the door to listen. The woman spoke:

"Yeah, you like that, Piggy?"

A muffled groan answered.

"You're my little bitch!"

More groaning.

"You better not be cumming yet!"

"Oh! Fuck, nearly!"

Holden rested his left hand on the door and held the camera with his right.

"Vera, you're getting the premium rate," he muttered. He twisted the door knob.

By the foot of the door was a greasy tarpaulin. Holden took another step in; the air was clammy and reeked of sweat.

In the centre of the office, Jerry stood tied by his wrists and ankles. A woman in black latex cracked a wooden panel against Jerry's bare ass. Two red raw circles glowed on each cheek like archery targets.

In front of Jerry, a pig's carcass lay lashed to a desk. Jerry groaned and thrashed in a mix of pain and ecstasy. His naked, pale body glistened with sweat as he jerked his hips, thrusting himself into the animal's corpse.

Holden raised his camera and cleared his throat. Wide eyes whipped round. SNAP! Gasping faces and the slack jawed pig were captured in a flash of white.

Holden slid an envelope across his desk. "As promised."

Vera took the envelope and slid the photograph out. Her eyes bulged. She placed a hand over her mouth.

She slipped the envelope into her purse. "Well, you've done a fine job, detective, thank you." She placed fifty dollars on the desk. "I guess that's why the bacon's been so salty lately."

I Love Bacon

Tom Fegan

Rose and I were planning a special Saturday morning breakfast at home; it was the ten-year anniversary of our marriage. Rose kept herself trim with walking and yoga as well as being an avid 'vegan'. She influenced me to follow suit. I was her second husband and she my first wife. Both of us past forty and her only child Nadine, a daughter, had chosen a career in the Army. She was almost grown when Rose and I married but appeared annually during her furloughs for a home visit.

I met Rose at work. She a technical writer for Norcom, a computer software company and I the company's Internal Security Director. It was during breakfast in the Norcom's employee cafeteria our first encounter happened. I was having my usual breakfast of two over easy, buttered toast and extra side of crisp bacon. Bacon; my only vice; I didn't smoke or drink, but bacon I relished on cheeseburgers, breakfast tacos, baked potatoes and pizza.

"How's your cholesterol?" she joked. It was a pleasant interruption as my attention directed to the tall, fit blonde with deep blue eyes. I invited her to join me after our brief introductions. She indulged in her own package of raw carrots, cauliflower and broccoli along with hot tea. She sighed. "I wished they had green tea. It's far better for you." Her pleasant personality and stylish appearance enamored me and the relationship began.

Rose was separated from Harold Gilstrap, the man who became my predecessor; once a successful sales manager for The Santa Fe Railroad Dallas office, he'd received a promotion as the Area Lead Manager with the company. This included a mandatory move to Houston, Texas. Harold rented an apartment and commuted back to Dallas on weekends. Vacations were spent with Rose and Nadine.

Rose had been a single mother before Harold appeared. A romantic tryst had left her pregnant and deserted by an irresponsible married man. She was grateful for Harold's support as a responsible parent and spouse. Although an avid sports fan, Rose soon weaned him off television sports, especially boxing, but understood him treating his clients to baseball, football, or basketball games.

One week she decided to surprise him with a visit to Houston. Nadine stayed with Rose's parents as she traveled to spend quality time with Harold. Her key to the apartment not only opened the door to the rental but a new life for her. She found him with another woman. Divorce was imminent, as was her keeping the house.

"I'm so happy with you," she declared through tear−filled, joy−filled eyes. Her precious smile spread warmth through me as we squeezed each other's hands across the table. "And I am equally happy that you understand I will always love Harold, but never leave you." I had lost count of the numerous times I'd heard this proclamation, but knew her feelings before marrying her. Harold may have broken their marriage vows, but prior to that had proven to be a good and responsible stepparent.

Our bond appeared secure. Her affectionate feelings for Harold were difficult to hear at times but sex was great and often. We spent ideal time together. I walked with her for exercise and though it took time, through her efforts readjusted my diet and lost weight. But I still missed bacon.

One dream I had, I ventured to my favorite diner where I could no longer go. An advertisement on its window stated, "All The Bacon You Can Eat For $10.00." Seduced by its message, I charged in and sat at the counter while a buxom waitress who'd always waited on me placed mounds and mounds of bacon before me non-stop. I shoved the delicious fried delicacy into my mouth as my taste buds engorged with the fantastic, familiar flavor. "Had enough, honey?" she grinned. I shook my head as more servings followed.

In another dream I woke up in the desert. I crawled through the sand, my tongue hanging out completely dry. I saw nothing but hills and hills of sand until I came upon a well; adrenalin kicked in as I pushed myself to my feet and ran towards this lifesaver. I dipped the bucket into the well and it came up filled with bacon. I ate the whole bucket and lowered it down for more.

Rose appeared from the kitchen with a platter piled with bacon. "Happy Anniversary!" she chimed. The platter was placed before me. I indulged myself, shoving the crispy fried pieces into my mouth.

It is give and take in matrimony; I gave up bacon mournfully. I still missed it. "I Love Bacon!" I shouted, shoveling more and more bacon into my mouth. "I love bacon. Give me more! Give me more!"

A violent shaking of my shoulders disrupted my moment with bacon. To my dismay I woke up to see my wife wearing a disturbed expression. "You were calling for bacon!" she groaned, her brow narrowing. "Whatever caused that?"

I sat up and shrugged, "I miss bacon." It was a heart—wrenched reply. Rose stood legs planted apart and shook her head. A sudden flush of rage filled me as she turned and reached for a tray set on the dresser. Breakfast in bed, our planned decade anniversary treat. The tray was filled with her homemade bread, egg whites, tomatoes, onions and avocado slices.

She gingerly placed the tray across my lap and stood back with her arms crossed. I could almost hear her thoughts, that if I didn't eat all my vegetables I would lose a privilege. But I already had! Bacon! I hurled the tray upwards. Rose threw up her arms. The airborne contents spilled down on the floor, on the bed, on the furniture, and on Rose.

With clenched fists I hammered on the mattress. Rose glared, hands hanging on her hips and avocado and tomato hanging on her scalp.

I roared a primal declaration, "I LOVE BACON! I LOVE BACON! I LOVE BACON!"

Exhausted, my face dropped into my palms as I wept.

Opening Procedure

Michael Webb

"You know that's bad for you, right?" she says. I am leaning forward, trying not to get any breakfast sandwich detritus on my shirt.

"Good morning to you too," I say as I chew. Her hair is pulled back, which makes her look severe and imposing. She sets a coffee on the counter near my elbow.

"Bacon is full of preservatives and bad fats," she says. She is a nursing student, and she thinks she is my mother.

"I have a doctor, thanks," I say, taking another bite.

"And you're going to keep him busy, eating like that." She looks at me disapprovingly.

"I have a mother, too," I say. "Well, had."

"Keep eating like a child, you'll see her again soon," she says. She swallows some more coffee.

"Do you have anything useful to say, or are you just going to think of ways I am a disappointment to you?"

"I can manage to do both," she says. She walks past me to the computer, wiggling the mouse to boot it up.

"How was your weekend?" I ask.

"Just...studying," she says.

"That sounds like an evasion."

"It does, doesn't it?"

The computer blooms to life, and she begins clicking and typing, her back to me. I don't want to mention it, but the words are out of my mouth before I can stop them.

"I'm sorry. Again."

"I know," she says. "And I've already forgiven you. Stop mentioning it."

"You don't have to. But can you tell me why?"

"I told you not to mention it," she says a little more firmly.

"You did."

"But if you must know," she says, "there are a couple of reasons. One, I work for you, which makes it complicated. But more importantly, I like you. I really do. And God knows, I wouldn't mind. It's been a while. But I do like you, honestly. And after I fuck someone, I always like them a little less."

She types in her password while I am wiping my mouth, and then slides over to push the button that starts our security gate sliding upwards. I watch her move and I don't say anything.

Lucky 8

Jonathan Slusher

I pulled back the tent flap and crawled out. The rain had stopped but wet pine needles were still stuck on my bare knees. I stepped into the darkness and unzipped. I shouldn't have had to piss in the middle of the night. I'd only drunk one beer. I was on a new medication and had to be careful.

"Some of my patients have said that it feels like a physical barrier that supports them, they can't drop into deeper depressive thoughts," the doctor had said.

He'd looked down through his bifocals at the laptop. He was probably looking at the clock. Time was almost up. Another two hundred and fifty bucks.

"Does it work for cutting out the anxious highs too?" I'd asked.

"Yes. It does," he'd assured.

It sounded too good to be true. They all had.

In the darkness, I listed the failed drugs in mid−stream: Zoloft, Lexipro, Ativan, Clonopin, Effexor, Symbalta, and Vraylar. Lamotrigine had a cool name, but I didn't get my hopes up. It was lucky number eight. I'd been on it for over a month and it hadn't done shit. I hoped the pee wasn't flowing in the direction of my bare feet.

I hadn't felt much of anything for a long time. Depression isn't a sadness. It is an apathy. I was pretty good at faking being ok, but internally I didn't feel much. Sometimes I felt super fucking anxious. Feeling nothing was preferable.

I didn't shake it off enough before zipping up and probably had a wet spot on my shorts. *Way to go, Dumbass.* The morning was going to suck regardless. It'd be all mud, feeding the boys, dealing with the trash, and packing up wet camping gear.

Daylight came quickly, I'd actually slept five or six hours. The boys were up and cooking over the fire. The sizzle rose higher with each piece of bacon placed into the pan. Cocooned, warm in an old down sleeping bag, the smell reached my nose. Two twelve year olds were out there cooking unsupervised. It sounded like they were cooking all three pounds at once.

I had my pants and shoes on before I noticed that I didn't have a morning headache.

We didn't greet each other, but just stared at the pan and the grease bubbling. They took turns using the tongs to move the strips around. There was already a cooked plateful piled three strips high. It was perfectly burnt.

"Hot," my son said.

I poked a piece anyway to feel how crispy it was.

"It's looks really good," I said.

"It'll change your life," said his friend.

"No shit?" I said. "It's definitely a start."

I grabbed a whole mouthful and chewed slowly. The combined sensation was a slap in the face. The bacon transcended the five senses. Suddenly, I was wide awake. I couldn't believe the boys had made breakfast all by themselves. Maybe the morning wasn't going to suck after all.

Water drops fell from the wet pines onto the needled forest floor, barely making a sound. Smoke from the fire had settled in the branches. A woodpecker worked away somewhere in the distance. Contentment, that was the feeling. It was a *feeling*.

When I looked over again both boys were laughing. I must have looked like a turbo Christian on a religious high.

All that was left in the pan was an inch and a half of bacon grease.

"Check this out, young grasshoppers." I raised my eye—brows.

I poured the grease onto the flames and lifted my hands to the sky as the fire rose into a five—foot inferno. They cursed and laughed as the flaming crescendo lasted for ten solid minutes. Pine branches swayed from the waves of heat.

It felt so gratifying to make them laugh. And that was another bona fide feeling. Maybe bacon and Lamotrigine was a winning combo. It had only been a few hours of feeling good. Maybe it wouldn't last forever. But I was on a roll.

I had a little momentum.

Food of the Gods?

Carolyn Cordon

Mmm, bacon, the mere word awakens my salivary glands and my tongue begins to explore my teeth for the salty taste of any possible bacon scraps! At the moment, I profess to being a meateater, but working hard to consume less meat, for myself, and for the planet.

But really, if humans were given the ability to discover the secrets of fire, surely one of the reasons for that was so we could turn big fat pigs into short lengths of bacon? The delicious scent of it, switching on various pleasure points in the brain, yum!

I like animals, I really do. I share my home with a dog, and have had dogs in my life for almost all of my adult time. But liking animals doesn't stop me from eating them. Some of them, anyway ...

Beef, lamb, chicken, crocodile, ostrich, I've tried all of them. Pig too, of course, in its various culinary forms. I've had tenderloins of pork, pork steak, roast pork, ham, and I've had bacon. Quite a bit of bacon.

This love of processed piggies brings me a sense of shame, when I think of the beasts, smart as a dog, and trainable, pet to some and fine pets at that, as far as I've seen. My neighbours behind my place once had pet pigs. The pigs were not too loud, or too smelly, they were fine. When I remember them again, my sense of shame grows.

I would certainly not want to eat a pet pig, but really, does that make up for my gluttony as I chow down on pancakes with banana and bacon, which is my fave way of having bacon? Rashers of bacon, served on pancakes, with sliced banana, and just the correct amount of maple syrup sprinkled on top, almost orgasmic!

Thinking about it, I'm wishing I could have that right now, the bacon with just the right amount of fat, crunch, and salt, the banana adding a delicious sweet flavour, the maple syrup with its hint of exotic 'foreignness', and pancakes to mop up and hold onto the divine combination of tastes, flavors, and textures. Bliss!

Hmm, if only. The closest place I know of, that could serve a plate of this, is too far away, at this time of the day, but soon, perhaps soon, bacon and I could meet up again for a little culinary treat. I'm so sorry pigs ...

Wet Meat

Kathleen Kenny

There is something dripping on my head; someone touching, creeping inside my costume leg. Slime falls from the roof, rises and drops in slick cycles. Yearning to go back, ask for a refund; I swim towards the big-armed women dressed like doctors. I wish to return to the cabin with the wire-mesh grill and cream paint, to where flesh begins. I want to unlock my possessions, give back the cotton sheet, cover my slippery feet.

Was my cabin number 59 or 65?

I was handed a wristband: 'Remember please this,' one of the women doctors said.

There are lanes of cabins and steam on my glasses. I've lost the wristband. I'm blind. My legs are metal frames devoid of flesh. I slide down jagged steps, find relief in the depth of a pool: no continental shelf. An underwater park, I rest on a tiled bench. Close by, bacon lips pull back revealing liquorice teeth. One plump hand offers a plate of pig-pink genitals.

This twilight world. The obsession of Hungary's landlocked. Szechenyi Gyogyfúrdó health spa, Budapest. One hundred and twenty fresh springs fondling hairy backs and necks, forests of ample flesh. Huge brass taps pummel arms and shoulders. Water gushes in spikes, unlocking knots of stress. Rushes of water on wet flesh. Condensation drips from high green ceilings. Murals of mould form beside frescoes. Swirls of moss surround rotund middles. There are domes and curves and girls in bikinis. A child clings to a parent; a couple intertwine, float over water, their legs enwrapped: one body, many limbs.

Following shapes of sailing flesh I squeeze into a clouded room of shared vapours and secrets and sex. The costumed and the naked. The disguised and the flagrant. I come unwelcome, unaccustomed to therapies of the dark. In this sauna full of breath, the pressure of inhaling presses on my chest.

Out.

Not knowing left from right.

Running darkened mazes, alternating shocks of hot and cold. Labyrinthine pools with green ceilings, green walls, green water. So many idyllic caves where taut young men with tiny loincloths laze together in green whirlpools.

I jump down the plughole with my pulled in belly and goose—fleshed legs. Hot vapours rise through cobbles, foot pools and footbaths. The toucher man is here again. I dissolve into the outdoors, wade to the centre of steam, the nub. Warming off in the hot open air, crowded flesh and chess sets pitch contesting intellects. Mountainous backs and wiggling tashes, fronted by faces of glass giving nothing away.

'Check!'

'Checkmate.'

Someone has won. His marble eyes float, fleet between the ears of his white swimming cap.

This is the life of the spa in Budapest: a world of mists and capers; fountains and springs bubbling up under the toes of my one numb, gashed foot. An injured yelp escapes. A gush of pain and condensation. Under the open night sky we mass like flies, float like angels, flaps fly over our languorous liquid eyes of Indian ink, hiding moonlight.

Blue Plate Special

Paul Beckman

Chas hates when Lydia yells at him when he's only having a morning taste so he goes to the fridge and takes out one of the three remaining generic beers.

Lydia, in her waitress uniform, rummages around her purse and finds her lipstick and ruby reds her lips. Chas hates the bright red Lydia favors but knows better than to say anything.

"If you lose this job," Lydia tells him, controlling her emotion, "just come home and pack and get your drunken ass out of here."

Chas assures her he's not going to lose his job. "I'm on the road crew starting today and all I have to do is hold a pole that says pass on one side and stop on the other and that's a union job paying close to twenty dollars an hour."

Lydia wants to know why he's sitting drinking and not on the job and Chas tells her he goes in at eleven and works until seven pm and then tries to explain between beer burps that it's a twenty-four hour a day contract.

Lydia offers to make him lunch and Chas thanks her and says a couple of BLT sandwiches will be fine and he walks over to the cupboard and takes out the Old Overholt and fills his flask telling her there's supposed to be a chill in the weather today.

Lydia watches this and tells him to make his own lunch and grabs her purse and heads off to the diner. It dawns on Chas he could have waited until Lydia left before filling his flask.

Lydia finishes her shift and sticks around for the employee meal—BLTs today.

James, the owner and cook, does a good job and always takes care of his girls. She knows he's sweet on her and loves her ruby red lipstick.

Lydia walks into her trailer and sees Chas still sitting in the kitchen passed out with the flask on its side and the BLT open on the table with all the B gone.

She walks back to the diner and sits at the counter having a cup of Joe and James comes out and says hello, I thought you left.

She tells him she no longer wants to live with and support a drunk and could she sleep on his couch.

James smiles at Lydia and tells her he's off in fifteen and will take her home.

In the morning James drives Lydia home to get her clothes and Chas is sitting on the stoop pounding a 40 when Lydia brushes by him and grabs her suitcase and packs it tightly and goes back out to James' car where Chas is calling James out for being a wife stealer and nothing but a fucking diner cook and he should get his ass out of the car and come fight him for Lydia.

Hearing this, Lydia tells Chas he's got a week to get out of their trailer and that week started yesterday.

Chas can't figure out why Lydia's so mad since he put in his full shift yesterday and got paid and they asked him back for today. He's just having his breakfast.

He walks over to James' car carrying his job. The car starts up, moves forward and Chas takes control of the driveway and holds the stick with **STOP** facing the car.

Mr Jenks' Shop

Christine Law

Brought up in the meat generation, I've become a meat and two veg person. It was interesting as a ten–year–old in the nineteen–sixties, to go with Mother to the butcher's shop. In those days, there wasn't a lot of talk about becoming "vegan". Television adverts showed the family sitting down at the table for Sunday lunch roast beef, potatoes and other fresh vegetables. There was also the advert with the little lion upon the eggs with people enjoying a good cooked breakfast of bacon, egg, sausages and beans.

There were three types of bacon: streaky rashers for breakfast; back bacon (thicker bacon with very little fat – good for bacon sandwiches with tomatoes); and horseshoe ham. How I remember that! Bacon shaped like a horseshoe that Mother bought for Father's evening meal. Horseshoe ham was the best bacon at two and eleven pence a slice. Mr Jenks the butcher sold all types of bacon, displayed on white trays in his shop window with the odd bit of greenery in between the trays for decoration. He also made his own pork and beef sausages to go with the bacon.

The butcher's shop was a small village shop, with a freezer room for the meat. Mr Jenks would cut the meat up himself. He wore a blue striped blood–stained apron over a white overall and carried a pencil behind his ear for jotting down orders. Usually the shop was full when it had six customers. Mr Jenks also did home deliveries in a blue Morris van. If he was busy his wife Mildred helped in the shop, her hair pushed up in a hairnet and wearing a white overall. She usually sliced boiled ham and cooked meats on a machine and wrapped up other items, including pork chops, joints of meat and bacon slices. Mr Jenks had a small saw and long sharp knives for cutting up the meat. These items were kept in a drawer when not in use.

Visiting the butchers shop, it did not frighten me. There were three small steps up to the door. The shop floor was always coated in sawdust, swept up at the end of business. Sometimes you saw the odd chicken hanging up in the shop window above the trays of meat; they usually ended up on someone's plate for Sunday dinner. Inside the shop there was a wire shelf for people to rest their bags upon. Above the shop was a blue striped blind for shading the eyes when looking in the window.

All the meat was cut and served up fresh on the day you bought it. Mr Jenks was noted for being a good butcher. I earned sixpence now and again for collecting the horseshoe ham for Father's evening meal. It was always interesting to see the ham and rashers of bacon being weighed on the scales with weights. I must say, now in my sixties, I have not done too badly on a meat diet.

Ernie is forced, or not, to make a difficult decision

Jennifer Rose

Ernie had a decision to make: to stay or go. He'd tried staying. It wasn't the *place*. The place was as good as any other, perhaps better, in some ways. He'd built a house here, raised his family here, made a few connections – a few. He was a quiet, reserved sort of bloke who liked to read and garden, took a bit of an interest in politics. The place suited him as well as any other might – more than the city would have, that's for sure.

It was his local church. He and Bess had been parishioners there the last ten years or so. The ageing congregation had welcomed them. He and Bess had been in their fifties at the time: the youth group. They'd made him a Warden. God knew, he hadn't actively sought it.

Recently things had changed. New brooms sweeping out old rubbish. Except it was not all rubbish. Not to the old timers. Sometimes things were the way they were for good reasons. 'If it ain't broke...' He'd felt for them and had spoken up – rather, he had asked questions.

He was still reeling from the other warden's email and the bishop's letters. He wanted to stay. But the bishop had suspended him. He was no longer deemed a 'safe' person. He had become part of the rubbish. He felt the push to go away.

Ernie wanted to do what was right. Don't we all? He got up, took his plate out to the dog's bowl, and scraped off his half–eaten eggs and bacon. He slipped into his study and got down on his knees (though he felt he'd already been there these past few months) and prayed.

There was no immediate answer. Just a kind of 'hold on' or 'I'm not saying anything, yet' kind of space. He wasn't worried or dismayed. He could wait. He could hold on. He wondered briefly how long the wait would be. He was sixty–five, so he had a few years up his sleeve before an eleventh–hour answer.

He eased himself up and ambled out to find his gardening hat, pocket radio and its plug–in earbuds.

'Bess love,' he called, 'I'll be out weeding the veggie patch.'

Bring Home the Bacon

Abha Iyengar

Stan did try to bring the bacon home. At least twice a week, he would go out to fetch it. On those days, his wife, Hilda, would look after the business of the shop he ran.

But every time he went to the pig market, he got lost among the sausages, the ham and the bacon; the smell overpowered him. He would just sit himself down on one of the tables in the marketplace, and ask to be served a small slice of everything that was on offer so he could decide what he wished to purchase. This is what he told the shopkeepers and sellers of the good old pig stuff.

And every time, he visited a different marketplace because he knew you could not fool the same sellers twice, especially not sellers of ham and bacon, for even though many had small, piggy eyes in fat faces (because everyone begins to resemble the products they sell, it was a known fact), they also had sharp calculating brains.

He had marketplaces marked out in his map at home, spread out on different days and different localities, and by the time he made a repeat visit anywhere, the people had forgotten him, because he had that nondescript type of face that could be easily forgotten after a while. And in their eagerness to sell, they sometimes may have remembered him and yet ignored that jolt of memory in the hope that this time for sure he would make a purchase.

Hilda seemed to be as gullible as the ham and bacon sellers, willing to be sold a story. After many years of living with him, she had yet to realize that he would never bring home the bacon. Every day, she used whatever vegetables she had to make the dinner. On the days Stan went to market, hoping to return with a fat pig, he came back empty–handed. But he also came back with no hunger in his stomach. He pretended to have a slice of the cauliflower and pea pie, or the vegetable stew, or the curried pumpkin or potato cutlets she served him. She was innovative for sure but after his day of feasting on bacon and ham outside, this was like fare for a pilgrim. Hilda could not understand his lack of appetite, after he had trudged so far and wide to different marketplaces, coming home looking flushed and wanting to sleep.

Stan often said, "I am so tired, but there seems to be no bacon available in the market at the price I want."

"Oh, you poor dear," she often said, "should I serve you some vegetables? I will have something piping hot for you from the oven soon..."

"Oh no, you eat it, Hilda. I am tired with all the bacon hunting. But I will try again, my dear, I won't give up..." He made such a sorry picture that she would run a hot water bath for him and hand him a cold sherry to drink in the bath while she slogged over the kitchen oven to prepare one more vegetable dish.

Over the years, she noticed how she was getting quite plump on vegetables alone because she could not bear to see food being wasted, and he was turning plumper because ... she could not understand why. In fact, he had begun to look quite like a pig, she thought one day, looking at him. And then she smelt one of his shirts before washing them and she could distinctly smell some piggyness in that sweaty smell.

Something within her stirred. She decided she would follow him one day instead of running the shop or doing the cleaning, dusting and washing. She could do with some travelling instead.

So when the next time he said, "Dearest, I am going shopping for some bacon, this time I hope we can have some for dinner," she smiled and waved him goodbye.

But before that, she asked, "Which market, dear?"

He was surprised at the question but shrugged and said, "Oh this time to Hockley's Farmers Market," and gave her the location of a market not too far from their home in Surrey.

Then she put on her best stockings and her best Sunday dress, wore her Sunday hat, and her sturdy walking shoes for she was a practical kind of girl, and she counted her pennies and put them in the inner pouch of her blue shopping bag and was on her way.

And so she saw her husband sitting eating ham and bacon at one shop and sausages at another, and then some chorizo at another, and some salamis at another, and then some pork ribs as well. She noticed he was not paying a penny for any of the food.

She had followed him closely and by now her mouth was watering and she walked up to a shop. The shopkeeper asked. "What you looking for, ma'am?"

Taken by surprise, she flushed, stepped back and said, "Oh, just some bacon, but I don't think…"

"Would you like a taste, ma'am? Decide after."

She nodded and sat at the empty table with the bacon she had been served. Her eyes closed in ecstasy at the first bite and then she quickly ate the rest.

"Hmm, it's okay," she said, "I'll try the other shop, and then…"

After a couple of hours, Hilda took the ride back home, had a shower, changed into a comfortable dress, put on her favourite TV show and relaxed. She did not have to cook any dinner today.

When Stan returned later in the day, she said, "Honey, you don't need to bring home the bacon anymore. I am going to get it from now on. Do serve me the sherry when you have had a shower."

No ham, no sausages, no bacon

Hazel Whitehead

'Here we are then, Greta. A lovely ham sandwich for lunch,' said Mollie, the Ward Hostess.

Greta sighed, half–closed her eyes and gripped the sheet on either side with knobbly hands. Tensing every muscle in her body, she managed, with much grunting, to pull herself up into a sitting position. She hated lying down. It was uncomfortable and it put her at such a disadvantage. She pointed to the sign fixed to the bedhead.

'I have a severe allergy to pork,' she said, the muscles in her neck twitching as they always did when she was frustrated.

'I know, my lovely. This isn't pork. It's ham.'

'And where does the ham come from?'

'Our normal suppliers, where we get all our meat.'

'Yes, but where does the supplier get the ham from? Which animal?'

Mollie hesitated, fiddled with her lanyard. Tests had always made her anxious.

Greta folded her arms and let out a deliberate sigh. She pursed her lips and spoke slowly and deliberately as if to a toddler.

'From a pig. It's pork. If I eat it, I might die. Or I might just scare you half to death as you watch me turn as red as a traffic light while I'm fighting for breath. Three or four minutes later, I will lose consciousness. Have you ever seen a corpse with a face so swollen they look like a giant guinea pig storing enough food for the whole winter?'

'We can't have that, can we,' said Mollie, swallowing hard. Greta heard a faint quavering in her voice. 'I think I get the picture. But you've got to eat — and I like a challenge.' She pulled a folded menu from her pocket. 'Let's see what else you might like. How about a cheese and bacon quiche with a bit of salad? Or a jacket with tuna?'

'Just for future reference,' said Greta, smoothing creases out of the blanket and folding her arms. 'I don't suppose you know where bacon comes from, do you?'

Mollie giggled and covered her face with her hands. 'Silly me. What am I like?'

Greta half–formed an answer and then thought better of it. She might be here for a day or two. No point in upsetting the hand that feeds you.

'Jacket with tuna will do nicely,' she said, forcing her mouth into a tight–lipped smile. 'No ham, no sausages, no bacon.'

It was difficult to be a patient and even harder to be patient. Every time, she had to go through the same rigmarole: pointing out the severity of her allergy, reminding them that some drugs are made from pork components, stressing that even using a contaminated knife could be enough. Maybe it would be easier not to tell them, eat the damned pork and get it all over with.

Greta moved the jacket potato around the plate, examining every small forkful for foreign bodies, swallowed a few teaspoons of ice cream and then closed her eyes. She kept them firmly shut every time she heard footsteps or trolley wheels approaching. She didn't want to buy a magazine or a snack and she wouldn't be there long enough to finish a library book. Anyway, she knew from bitter experience they were either simpering romances or self–improvement manuals and she was too old for either.

She certainly didn't want the Chaplain telling her Jesus loved her so she snored loudly when she caught a glimpse of a dog collar but he was only showing a new member of the Chaplaincy Team the ropes, pointing out the mandatory sanitisers and the small whiteboards by every patient's bed which gave critical information, introducing him to members of staff. It was five o'clock. A ridiculous time to serve the final meal of the day. A cheerful but unfamiliar face appeared at the side of the bed, swivelling the table over her bed. Where was Mollie?

'Evening, Greta,' said the cheery voice. 'Ready for tea? Rice with sweet and sour pork. Looks yummy.'

The rice just missed the Chaplain's grey jacket but scattered far and wide across the floor. Unfortunately, his new colleague, Rabbi Daniel, was right in the line of fire as the glutinous, sweet and sour orange mess with its insipid chunks of meat flew across the bed straight into his face.

'I said: No ham, no sausages, no bacon!' she yelled. 'And that means no pork.'

She glared at the Rabbi as if he was to blame. 'If you're really wanting to do good, I'd like a cream tea with Cornish clotted cream and strawberry jam. And a half decent cup of Earl Grey. Decaffeinated.'

Take a Letter

Mark Bridge

Sorry, mate. Look, I know you're the housekeeper and this really isn't your job but would you mind making a few notes and drafting me a letter? It's just that my fingers are too cold. Literally chilled to the bone, I think. Thank you. So, yeah... in fact, let's put that in the letter. No, somewhere in the middle. A bit obvious otherwise. Usual stuff at the beginning. Arundel House, Highgate, year of our lord 1626. Okay, down to business. Dear Tom. Actually, best do it properly. Dear Lord Arundel. Remember how Pliny the Elder died in the name of science by getting too close to the eruption of Vesuvius? It seems like I'm going to suffer the same fate, except I've been killed by a frozen chicken. Fine, I'll write my own sodding letter if you're going to laugh. Keep a straight face and there's an extra sixpence for you at the end of this. Okay. So I went out for a ride in the snow, which inspired me to try an experiment with a chicken. Hmm. That's not a smirk, is it? Turns out I was right: chilling meat really does preserve it. Shame everything all went a bit belly–up from that point. Pun intended. Feel free to chuckle. Don't know whether I picked up a bit of food poisoning or if I shouldn't have opened the second bottle of port at breakfast but I started throwing up in the carriage. Absolutely couldn't face the journey home; that's why I stopped here. Oh, we've had some fun in our younger days, me and your boss. Shame he's not around at the moment. I reckon this is a good place to say how carefully you've looked after me. What? No, in the letter. A good place in the letter. You've done him proud. Best bed and all that. A bit damp to start with but it wouldn't be the best bed if it was used all the time, would it? Exactly. That'll do nicely. Perhaps something to explain why you've written it, not me. Kind regards, Francis Bacon. Hey, if you're going to laugh at my name as well, you can kiss that sixpence goodbye. Knowledge is power, sunshine.

The Hostage

John Notley

Some time back my daughter Sally spent many years moving from country to country to be with her husband, a Frenchman, whose job with an airline involved a new posting every four years. It was my good fortune to be able to visit many places I would not normally have considered. One of these countries was Benin in West Africa.

For those whose geography is a little rusty, Benin is a small strip of a country sandwiched between big brother Nigeria to the East and Togo to the West. It is a former French colony so French is widely spoken there. It is also known for its association with Voodoo.

The main town where I stayed several times is Cotonou, a busy port on the coast. Its Catholic Cathedral, Notre Dame, is about the only building of any interest, but I was more often drawn to The Livingstone Bar, used by many of the expats, and became friendly with a local African gentleman. There, over a couple of glasses of the local lager "La Beninoise" and a bit of gossip, I got to know Calixste. Calixste, a stocky man with a round smiling face, reminded me a bit of a young Louis (Satchmo) Armstrong. He had a souvenir stall not far from the bar, dabbled in real estate and was known locally as a wheeler—dealer.

Many a night he took me on the back of his motorbike to

the seedier areas of the city where we would drink in dark, dingy bars. I was usually the only white guy in the place. I always felt safe with my friend since he was well known by many people and quite able to take care of himself (and me) if need be.

One of my favourite pastimes while staying in Cotonou was to have a full body massage and my daughter knew a particular young lady who had a salon nearby. On the day in question I arranged for Sally to pick me up after my massage and take me back to her villa.

I waved goodbye to my lovely Beninoise masseuse and left the small single storey building which served as her salon. Despite my 65 years I felt as fit as one thirty years younger after one hour of her expert ministrations. The afternoon sun was beating down hot as ever on the galvanised tin roofs of Cotonou and dust rose round my sandalled feet as I walked to my daughter's waiting car.

I climbed in beside Sally. We pulled away along the dusty track but within a few yards the car's wheels bogged down in a deep rut spinning frantically in the sand.

"I'll have to get help," Sally said irritably as she stepped out of the car.

Just then a gang of four or five youths sauntered past us. Sally approached the one who appeared to be the oldest, maybe seventeen, and asked in French if they would help to get us moving again.

The older boy took the wheel while three more pushed from behind and the car slowly moved forward with me sitting beside the driver. Sally thanked him, withdrew a couple of notes from her bag and put her hand on the door handle.

"That's not enough," said the boy aggressively

"It will have to do," Sally replied in exasperation. "I don't have any more on me, until I get home."

"OK, leave the old man here and go back for more."

I sat unconcerned, unaware of what had been said.

Sally looked around nervously for some support. Relief seemed to be at hand as she heard a shout and spotted a large African lady bustling towards our car. She carried a small baby strapped to her back.

The three younger lads had already seen her and wisely made off at speed in the opposite direction.

The lady stopped beside the car, her ample chest heaving, and breathed deeply.

Sally quickly explained the situation to her in French, which she seemed to understand. She pushed Sally aside, thrust her head through the driver's window, shouting at the boy behind the wheel. She then pulled open the door, reached in and grabbed his t—shirt with one hand while slapping his face with the other. She ordered him out of the car and waving her arms and shouting at him, she started to push him away. The baby on her back joined in and was bawling loudly as they left the scene.

The hostage was free.

I innocently asked my daughter, "How do I thank the women who saved my bacon?"

The Time of Bacon

Tracie Lark

Every hero's story includes a journey, archetypes, and conflict. I was the hero. I grew up in an ordinary world, The Time of Meat and Two Veg. They were simple times with simple pleasures. When I got my call to adventure, I was as naive as a boiled potato. My mentor wafted into my life one day and gave me the confidence to cross the threshold, where I landed in The Time of Soups and Broths, and that's when I first met my shapeshifting nemesis.

It appeared to me, subtly, a mere warning, tantalising my tongue in salty stock, so I devoured it. Fear and suspense reside in the void where the mind wields potential consequences, more so than in the use of power, I realised.

The more I consumed my enemy, the more present that enemy became. I traveled to The Time of The Entrée in pursuit, intending to overcome and destroy. There it was, choking a flushed prawn and drowning its head in white sauce, so I devoured it once again, satisfied – but not for long.

Every hero has their weakness, and I actively pursued my enemy, knowing its trick, how it would continue to appear through time, in different forms, alluring me, and I let it.

I reached The Time of the Main Course and there it was, belly first staring me down from underneath its salted, crackled cape. We fought the eternal conflict yet again. I chewed through and in the end, I won once more.

I'm just a human hero, and I could feel myself getting older and slower and I knew that one day I would have to return home, albeit a changed being, but I felt I would never be able to live a normal life again since I crossed the threshold from my ordinary world. My mentor advised me, proceed and you will become the hero of the ages, and then warned me that I couldn't give up now, for there is no way to go back in time.

So I boldly marched on through The Time of Desserts where I knew I would be safe: there was no way my enemy could reach me here in this sweet oasis. I trudged along through the Banana Cake Swamp, wading through sticky maple syrup, avoiding choc chip hotspots. Just as I was bending my body forward, slurping myself from banana quicksand, there it appeared, in glazed chips, broken and sweet but everywhere. I consumed, devoured, I licked its salty sweetness from my lips and crossed finally, into The Time of Aperitifs.

That was it, I had won! Lemoncello rained upon my shining soul. I caught my reflection in the sweet and sour clouds and I knew it was time to heal after a lifetime of eternal conflict.

I slept, I bathed, I meditated, I flossed. I sawed that string back and forth, dredging my gums, and lo and behold, from within a cavity, it appeared again: my shapeshifting enemy, Bacon. I hung Bacon from my finger and stared it down, face to face and said, I will not let you control me anymore, and I flicked Bacon from my finger, down the plughole, where it slurped through to the drains of Hell.

These many years later, I sit in my old skin and bones, frail and frumpy, and I realise that I never successfully abolished Bacon, for Bacon had shapeshifted into its most powerful form;

I didn't realise that Bacon had been inside of me this whole time. What was meant to be an external conflict was truly internal; I am my own worst enemy.

My heart is struggling as Bacon strides through my veins commandeering Captain Salty Cholesterol in staggering pulps. Okay, you win, Bacon. I could never beat something as formidable as you. I'm dying, I know.

My mentor appeared again in a light at the end of my bed, dressed as a nurse. You can live, you know. There is a way. My mentor placed a tray of Meat and Two Veg before me and that's when I learned that a hero can travel back in time, for Time is subject to perception, and the threat of losing it is just like that of fear, more powerful in its promise. Much like the alluring aroma of an adventurous meal.

Pigs Might Fly

Doug Jacquier

There's Bacon and there's Bacon. In fact, a whole shedload of Bacons dot the British historical landscape. One of their claims to fame was their propensity to promise to pay for things with money they didn't have and marrying to obtain other people's money. In that sense, bringing home a Bacon then did not bring forth rejoicing like it does today. It is rumoured that the clan had a certain tendency to bed–hopping and that the lineage may have included more bastards than a loan sharks' convention.

But let us repair to more modern times and that artistic enfant terrible, Francis Bacon. If I may digress momentarily, Francis' grandfather, Anthony, in the best Bacon tradition, emerged from a debtors' prison to seek out investors to support the obviously insane idea of building a British colony in South Australia.

That obviously planted a seed in the minds of some of the family tree, to the extent that Francis' father, 'Eddy' Bacon, was born in Adelaide to a British father and an Australian mother and his siblings continue to have roots in Australia. However, Eddy reverted to type and married a British coal heiress, scuttled off 'Home' and they spawned the said Francis and three other progeny.

Poor Francis had a largely miserable childhood, mostly as a result of his father's abhorrence of anything smacking of femininity or homosexuality in his son. At one point he had a stablehand attempt to whip this stain out of Francis' system. Suffice to say he was unsuccessful.

Francis ran away to London as a young man, surviving on an allowance from his mother. It would seem the only arts he would pursue for many years were drinking and gambling. But then he discovered art and gradually art discovered him and his artistic excrescences made him wealthy in his own lifetime, that rarest of achievements, and it became de rigueur to bring home a Bacon.

Of course after his death in 1992, the monetary value of his works soared, and one has sold for over $140 million. The artistic value of his twisted and depressing world view remains the same, i.e. a con job of monumental proportions.

It would seem that the apple never falls far from the tree in the Bacon dynasty. Wouldn't it be fitting if these massive profits were returned to the descendants of those their family ripped off over the years? Pigs might fly.

Forecourt Flowers

Jessica Joy

They sit in the corner of the restaurant: tight smiles over the rose glow of red wine, while the waiter arranges their cutlery. In an amber glass jar, the candle sputters as the wick sinks into the well of wax, a bitter smell of sulphur left between them.

I gave him all of me; every wave of emotion, every tsunami of desire, every swell of my love, until the reservoir of feelings burst its banks. Now it all seeps into the barren ground. All the days we spent in deep and earnest conversation; all the hours pressed to each other's skin, all the minutes snatched in lunch times, intervals and taxis. I thought we were bound forever. I thought he knew me.

He watches her profile in the dim light as she stares through the window into the night. Or stares at their reflection in the black glass.

She feels it too, he's sure, the all—consuming certainty of his undying love for her. He can see her tremble under his unblinking stare.

Words cannot express the depth of the physical pain his yearning causes; the tightness in his heart, the knot in his stomach. The flowers that lie between them on the table were a spontaneous gesture, inspired. She glances at them and sighs. He is certain their poignancy is not lost on her: white chrysan—themums for the truth of his feelings, carnations for how his

132

heart aches for her, roses and tulips pledge his love and one large daisy for hope, hope for their future together.

And beautifully presented in blue polka–dot paper, the same shade as the dress she wore on their first meeting. The flowers are perfect.

I'm going to have the bacon–wrapped chicken. He's paying.

She is radiant. He can't contemplate food.

Moving the blooms to the empty chair to her side, her fingers linger a moment on the velvet petals of the rose.

Their eyes meet, reflecting only the harsh glare of the overhead lamp.

She loves them.

I hate them. Cheap, tacky last–minute gesture.

I'll ask her now. He touches his pocket to feel the round edge of the small box.

I'm breaking up with him. She scrapes back her chair and can't distinguish between the shrill scream of wood on vinyl tiles and the one in her head.

'I want more than forecourt flowers.'

Home for the Holocaust

E. M. Stormo

Before I reach the checkpoint, the dogs smell my infection. They bark through the window and scratch at the door. The guards stay in the booth while I step out of my car for a once—over. I can tell by their brown coats they're Germans: the dogs, not the guards. They sniff up and down my legs like I got bacon in my pockets and cancer in my crotch, but mine is a mental infection, undetectable to the nose. I can't smell anything myself. The air is too thick up here. The guards won't come out, so they motion me through the gate. I'm free to go, but not to return.

Mom lives only one hundred miles from the city, but it takes me hours to drive through multiple checkpoints with mild harassment each stop of the way. The various police, statees, counties, and townies, all subject me to the same clown routine: throat—clearing, mic check, octaves, low to high and back down. My lows sound suspicious, as they should after an after—noon of such froggery, but nobody wants to get close enough to put the zip ties on me.

"I used to be a smoker," I explain, slightly spitting out the words onto the road.

The policeman rears and shields his face. "Talk into your shirt!"

"Sorry." The word drips down my chin in a rivulet. "Rivulet of drool," writes the bad poet while sitting back to collect his government check. I don't pay taxes, nor do I make enough to be on welfare. I'm nothing but an animal with a social security number. A germ with a face attached.

Once I arrive in town, a bike gang of masked bandits circle my car, but they ride off after they see my plates. Yeah, that's right, kids. I'm from the city and I've come to infect your town. Stay away from me and my dirty brain.

Her house is upstate in the mountains, which would've been the perfect spot to hole up and hunker down, but it is not the house I grew up in. It belongs to my stepfather. He peeps through the blinds as a toy dog bounces next to him. The door swings open and the two of them greet me, one towering tree trunk of a man and one yappy fluffball.

I wave from afar, thinking that'd be it, but the old fool comes closer to shake hands. Does he not know I'm infected? His hands are discolored like a body dumped in the river. I don't want to shake, so I offer my elbow to bump.

"What's that? I ain't sick. Don't hand me a cowardly body part like an elbow. Shake my damn hand."

I extend my arm and he shakes the entire limb while the fluffball sniffs around my ankles.

"Your mother's taking a swim out back." He smells his hand with a smile. "I'm gonna wash up for dinner."

I approach the perimeter of the pond with caution. Mom practices her backstroke in a lightly colored onesie. Her clothes are hanging from a willow branch, but it still doesn't register. Only when she gets out do I realize she was skinny-dipping. Her naked body bears the same discoloration as my stepfather's hands. She gives me an air—hug, squeezing her breasts together. Her pubis drips. I can't believe I used to live here.

"You made it, finally," she says.

"They wouldn't let us leave yesterday," I lied.

"Well, at least you're not coughing. Are you getting enough zinc?"

"I'm not sick."

That doesn't stop them from seating me at the far end of the dinner table, the way a royal family eats. Mom's chicken soup is extra spicy and pops open my sinuses. I snuff every sneeze, using my finger as a small mustache.

She eyes my throat suspiciously while I sip in silence. My stepfather chews his soup, but he doesn't get in trouble. They're immune to each other.

"So, your mother and I have talked about it, and we'd prefer you to stay in the barn."

"What about the guest room?"

"That's Madga's room."

The fluffball yaps in agreement.

"What am I gonna do?"

Mom laughs open—mouthed, tongue swirling. "You don't do anything anyway."

The fluffball hops in my stepfather's lap and places her paws on the table. "We put Netflix in there."

"Aren't there animals?" I ask.

He feeds Magda from the same spoon. "We got rid of the piggies."

"There might be a barn cat who hangs around," Mom says. "You can use the hose to wash off."

"Why not the pond?"

136

Mom shifts in her seat. She looked more comfortable naked. "I'd prefer you didn't."

"Why not?"

"Listen to your mother." Now he's kissing the dog on the lips.

So I'd stay in the barn indefinitely. I would not infect the house or the pond. Just sit on my haystack, watch Netflix, and slowly rot in place. They'd leave my bones in a pile to show off when company comes over. Look, there's my son's bones. He got down with the sickness. Nobody knows where his brain went. It's stored in the same freezer as all the missing brains, right next to JFK.

The moon peeps through a hole in the roof, but it won't come any closer. It's a night of bad poetry. Guano smeared on everything. Birds or bats, doesn't matter. I could cover myself in shit. Nobody would care. I'll never touch anyone again. This is what I've come to. A middle—aged child living at home, cast out with the animals.

In my bout of self—pity, I don't notice a pair of eyes shining at the other end of the barn. They move closer. She smells it. Like a hospital kitty, she knows my death draws near. Or maybe I'm cured and the disease has run its course. Whatever the reason, she lays herself down next to me, so I don't have to sleep alone.

Rebellion

Sarah Jane Justice

For me, hating bacon was an act of rebellion.

I was the child who talked back into ears that were stubbornly deaf to my voice. With opinions growing faster than the hairs on my head, I loathed the inevitability of having them ignored. No matter what volume my voice could reach, I was met with a shush and a pat on the head, if I received a response at all.

I fought back with a statement that could never be ignored.

"Ugh, bacon?" I screwed up my nose, "I don't like bacon."

The room of grown-up voices crashed into immediate silence as all eyes fell on me.

"I beg your pardon?" my father rose from his seat, suddenly desperate for my response. "What do you mean you don't like bacon?"

"I don't know," I shrugged, exaggerating my nonchalance as I pushed the plate away. "I just don't like it. You can have it if you want."

My comments on war, politics, or the environment would be left to droop down the couch cushions like a five-cent piece, but my rejection of bacon would always be heard.

"How can you not like it?!" my mother would snap.

"It's delicious!" my uncle would throw his hands in the air. "It's objectively delicious!"

"You can't dislike it for no reason," my teacher would shake her head. "There's nobody who just doesn't like the taste."

"Well I don't," I would answer, calm in the reflected glow of irrational frustration. "You must be wrong about that, I suppose."

As the torrents of rage subsided, people began to accept my refusal to worship their porcine God. With little more than a disgruntled shrug, they grew accustomed to leaving the bacon rasher off my mixed grill.

In the face of acceptance, all acts of rebellion should leave with a final blow. A move that hits with enough driving force to ensure a lasting impact, no matter what else might be forgotten.

At the end of a family dinner, one last, leftover crisp of salty meat was left to stray on a serving plate. When no eyes were aimed at me, I picked it up and set my teeth to crunch, as audibly as they were made to do.

"Wow, this is really good," my young voice boomed into older ears. "Why didn't anyone tell me that bacon is so delicious?"

To this day, I have never felt so powerful.

In the Pursuit of Bacon

Cheryl Ferguson Bernini

She woke one morning, a stranger in a foreign land. It was her choice to move away, but now she had second thoughts. The nagging sentiment that she had somehow made a terrible mistake did not grow from the family or friends left behind or from the fact she lived thousands of miles away. It intensified because of various physical or material things she gave up and left behind.

Understandably, everyday life would not be the same. Relocating to another country, she had transferred across the Atlantic to Italy, bringing with it many challenges. Some things, more fitting to say absolutely everything, would not be like home. The language, the laws, add to the mix work, meeting new people, and the list continued on, rolling open like a mega roll of toilet paper.

Take, for instance, morning dining. It did not entail cooked meals like those she ate on weekends with her family. No, Italians preferred a more dine and dash method. A sweet brioche followed by a shot of espresso, and into the rat race of life they ran. However, when the craving for the comfort of sentimental memories and a bite of the salty delight became unbearable, she could do nothing else. The hunter initiated the pursuit of a prey already captured, packaged, and ready to consume.

Searching locally, store by store, the glorious strips she could not find. The longing, the yearning, for the succulent meat created for this woman a quest. Although not directly involving a threat of life or death, she felt some days as though she could not go on. Thoughts overflowed with deprivation, of not having access to the genuine thing, and it made her question existence while despair painted her an even gloomier portrait.

One day, she met a man who would one day become her husband. In him, she found a confidante, someone she could divulge her deepest thoughts and secrets to, one of which was her insatiable hunt for bacon. However, the Italian didn't fully understand this odd adoration since he had never before savored the celebrated salt−cured pork.

From his TV viewership, he knew only through this fictitious world of the wondrous foods on which Americans feasted. He questioned his girlfriend, wanting to understand a person's proclivities and his or her tastes. After some time together, he asked if she would prepare him dishes, like pancakes and French toast, if she had available the correct ingredients.

And she did. Yet the plates, with sausage links filling the ceramic void, lacked something essential. She missed having that delectable treat; and, now that she couldn't have it, she wanted it even more. Unbeknownst to her companion, she experienced a despondency when eating those breakfasts, never fully satisfied without her beloved bacon served on the side.

While on their weekly journeys, either near or far, the duo came across new supermarkets to explore. With hope in their hearts, they stopped and inspected the refrigerated shelves in each new locale. Italian−based, French−based, German−based shops, they investigated them all. However, they always left downtrodden and empty−handed. No one carried the product for which they hungered.

In a vain attempt, they tried every type of meat, Speck (a flavorful, thinly sliced ham), pancetta affumicata (cured smoked pork belly), and guanciale (pork jowls), hoping one would satisfy their desire for the actual thing. However, their proximity in description only made them veiled imposters, imitations of the crown jewel. They continued the search for this impossible−to−find treasure, futile attempts that nearly broke the pair's spirits.

When they married, the couple traveled to the United States. It was there that her Italian husband not only discovered for himself a love of bacon but where he came to understand the significance behind her unyielding need for the authentic pork product. Each morning, they stopped at a local diner or restaurant and feasted on a full American breakfast. Along with the eggs, pancakes, or French toast, there was always that tried− and−true delicacy sitting beside it, lightly cooked or extra− crisp. They considered a day without bacon a somber and wasted day.

It came in flavors like maple or hickory−smoked, as delicate ribbons or hearty slabs. It didn't matter as long as it was present. So many varieties with just as many recipes in which to use it. Accompanying a meal, piled high on a burger, or sprinkled on a salad, they awarded it the honor of being the most versatile foodstuff.

The husband, after a month's holiday, declared in his accented English, "I am the Baconator! I will be back." His wife joked, borrowing more from Latin than Italian, "The

Romans and Bacchus have nothing on us. We've eaten bacon every day. Welcome to our personal month's long baconalia."

As they sat in the booth on their last day, they savored each morsel as if it would be their last, pondering what life would be like without the streaky treat.

It was almost as if fate intervened when they both declared, "I love bacon." He licked his greasy lips as she patted her oily fingertips on a paper napkin. From across the table, they stared deep into one another's eyes.

But, what would become of it once they returned to a desolate, bacon–less home? In desperation, they checked online to see if it could be ordered and delivered. The pursuit would continue, but at least they could chase the craving together.

Save My Bacon

Matt Cowan

"How the hell are we going to market this?"

"What are you talking about? It's *bacon*. It markets itself!"

"Yeah, well..."

"Don't tell me you're having second thoughts."

"No..."

"You promised we'd do this together."

"I know."

"Then what's the problem? There's clearly still a demand for it. After we all went veggie, then vegan, then synthetic, *bacon* is the one thing people still miss from before."

"Yeah, but..."

"But what?"

"Well, look at it!"

"...What's wrong with it?"

"Are you kidding? It's *disgusting*."

"But, it doesn't feel pain."

"You sure?"

"Of course I'm sure! What the hell are you suggesting? We stopped eating animals when we were able to understand their thoughts."

"*Most* of us..."

"Then, when we understood that eggs, and even plants felt pain, we went synthetic – eating the same flavourless gruel grown in vats. This is just the next step."

"It seems like a step backwards."

"Not at all. This is the future."

"But, it's alive."

"No, that's the great thing about it. It's really not. It has no central nervous system, no bones – you'd be surprised how little of the animal you need. Just the guts, and the flesh. And the heart and lungs. Oh, and a mouth and a sphincter, of course."

"Of course..."

"Try some."

"Not, it's okay."

"Please, I insist."

"Oh, all right... Mm. Tastes good."

"See? I told you... You don't seem impressed."

"No, no. I *am* impressed, it's just..."

"What?"

"Oh, God..."

"What?"

"Where's the bathroom?"

"Down there, to the left."

"Thanks."

"Feeling better?"

"Mm."

"Want another piece?"

"*Ugh.*"

"Only joking. It takes a few goes before you're able to keep it down."

"How many times have you eaten it?"

"Oh, more than I can count. I can eat some now, if you want."

"*No!* No, that's okay. I'll take your word for it."

"It's called neuroplasticity. You have to change your brain's structure a bit."

"A bit? Jesus, you must really like bacon."

"That's what I'm telling you: *everyone* loves bacon. We're going to make a fortune!"

"Hmm... We need to hide *that*, pretend it's synthetic."

"Wait, isn't that illegal?"

"No, no, I'll work it out. We can explain to the WHO that it's not alive, that it is, in a sense, synthetic. Might take a few months of lobbying, but it can be done. We'll have to come up with a name. Fake Bacon? Facon...? God, it's hypnotic. Uh, I think I'm going to..."

"Don't look. But, wait, the whole point is that it's *not* synthetic."

"People haven't eaten living things in so long, I'm not sure how they'll cope with... *this*. Our best way forward is to make them think it's grown in a vat."

"But it *is* grown in a vat."

"You know what I mean."

"So, you'll do it? You'll help us market it?"

"Yeah, sure. Like you said, there's a huge demand for this. We're going to make a lot of money."

"*Yes!* Thanks, man. I knew I could count on you. And don't worry: you'll get free bacon for the rest of your life for doing this!"

"...No, thanks."

A Fridge Full of Bacon

Jane Andrews

I gazed at the fridge in disbelief. A week ago, I had emptied the fridge before my husband and I went on holiday, but the fridge was definitely not empty now. Upon the previously bare shelves sat a packet of butter (we only ever buy sunflower margarine), a block of lard (ditto, olive oil) and what looked like enough bacon to set up a truck stop.

"Did you buy any milk?" My husband joined me at the open fridge door and peered inside. "What the hell is that?" he asked, pointing to the mound of dead pig. (I should point out at this stage that we are both staunch vegans.)

"Someone," I said, "has broken into the house while we were away and filled our fridge with animal products."

Matt looked at me sharply. "You're joking, right?"

"I'm afraid not," I said, waving my hand at the damning evidence and wondering whether, in the short time we'd been away, someone had founded a Meat Liberation Front and was trying to make us all compulsory carnivores. Perhaps I should get Matt to google local bacon terrorist activities?

But my husband was shaking his head and frowning. "She wouldn't..." I heard him mutter. "Not after I told her..."

"You know something about this!" I said in surprise.

He looked sheepish. "Well, not exactly... But I've got a pretty strong suspicion."

And so the story came out of how his mother had rung him the week before we went away and asked if she could housesit for us while we were gone.

"Why didn't you say yes?" I asked, thinking that at least the old lady would have been some sort of deterrent against burglars. (My mother–in–law's a formidable woman and has been known to wrestle a Hell's Angel to the ground when she thought he was after her handbag.)

He looked awkward. "Well," he said slowly, "I told her no because I had a feeling she wanted to use our house as a love nest."

I goggled at the idea of his parents getting down and dirty in our hot tub while we were away. "But I thought your dad's just had a hip replacement!" I argued.

Matt looked even more embarrassed at this. "I don't think she was intending it to be for her and my dad," he whispered. "I think she's got a bit on the side!"

Now, I don't know about you, but the idea of a woman in her sixties writhing around in extra–marital passion is not an image I want in my mind. Even now, it still makes me feel queasy if I think about it. What was even worse was that I knew Matt was just as perturbed as I was. "Do you think..." – he could hardly get the words out, poor love – "do you think the bacon and butter were part of some bizarre sex game?" (I vowed there and then that we would never watch *Last Tango in Paris* or *9½ Weeks* ever again.)

For the rest of the evening, we were too traumatised to speak any more.

It was a day or two later when a kindly neighbour provided another piece of the jigsaw puzzle. I was carrying out the garbage when Robin from next door called out. "We gave your mum the key."

"Pardon?" I felt confused.

"Your mum – when she was here last week. She said you'd promised to leave a key out for her, but she couldn't find it – so we gave her your spare."

"She's Matt's mum, not mine," I replied automatically. Then curiosity got the better of me and I asked, "Did she have anyone else with her?"

"Oh, you mean your father–in–law?" Robin didn't seem to realise the enormity of this conversation. "Nice chap – we had a good chat about bikes. Said he's got a Harley at home."

"He wasn't on crutches, then?"

I was hoping Robin would contradict me, but instead he laughed. "He's the fittest bloke for his age I've ever seen – and he couldn't keep his hands off your mother–in–law!"

So Matt had been right: his mum was messing around with another man – and she'd chosen our house for her not–so–secret assignation! Full of righteous indignation, I marched back inside. Who knew what they'd been up to in our home? I was going to have to strip all the beds and bleach every available surface!

By the time Matt came home from work, I'd calmed down enough to think things through. I was still mad at Mrs McKenzie for using our house without permission; but a part of me almost admired her for having such energy at the age of sixty–five. After all, I reasoned, it wasn't as if her husband was the innocent party in all this – Matt had told me on several occasions what a philanderer his dad had been when Matt was growing up, so perhaps it was time his wife got her own back. "Sauce for the goose," I muttered to myself.

Something told me Matt wouldn't be too happy if I confirmed his suspicions, though. So, I did what any loving wife would do and lied.

"By the way," I announced casually, "I've solved the mystery of the bacon."

I waited for his response.

"Did you ring my mum?" he wanted to know.

I shook my head. "I didn't need to. Robin next door said he and Katy put the food in our fridge as a welcome home present – you know they had our spare key."

Matt's face flooded with relief. "Thank goodness I didn't ring her," he said fervently.

I knew then that we would never speak of the incident again.

"Oh, and one more thing..." I wasn't sure how he'd react to this one, "I thought I might cook that bacon for supper tonight."

After all, it's hard to keep on being a vegan when a packet of bacon is calling to you from the fridge.

My Father Loved Bacon

Iris N. Schwartz

Canarsie, Brooklyn, New York, summer, 1962. Limp morning (pre–a/c). Mother in Smithfield*–pink robe scorched scrambled eggs til they stuck to iron pan, fired up bacon til smoking strips begged for mercy, or for Marlboro onesies. Scraped cast iron w/spatula til ferrous metal speckled eggs & air redolent of burnt dreams.

One godforsaken summer night, calf's liver downright edible — no doubt due to unctuous oinker. Pig strips whip–snapping crisp; purple onion shreds incinerated beside them. Strips waved white napkins, onions offered teeny falsettos: "We give up, we give up, we give up!"

Thirty years on I recall bacon's globule–rich smell; on paper towels, telltale spots — wet, shining jewels. Mother, eighty–five, builds charred BLT now & again. Father didn't make it past sixty–two, because ... well, you read the title, right?

* Smithfield, Virginia, USA is home to Smithfield Hams.

The Space Between 12 and 1

Len Kuntz

This is the fourth time in four days Sis says she's going to do it.

She's just made eggs for breakfast and claimed the bacon screamed at her as it was sizzling in the grease—popping pan. She said the bacon called her a murderer. In a calm tone that made my skin pucker, Sis claimed the bacon said she should do it—kill herself, as atonement.

Mom says Sis is just a mixed—up cunt, that she tries too hard to figure out the meaning of life when life is mother—fucking pointless. Wake up already, Mom says, life's a heartless bitch. Take a peek.

Mom says Sis should stop eating her hair and eat the god damn bacon and eggs. Mom's only wearing her seafoam bra and balloon panties again, sweat from the early August heat gleaming on the stubble of her chin. What? she shouts, flinging the yellow—slickened spatula at the wall clock, nailing the blank space between 12 and 1.

Before she stomps down the trailer hallway, Mom says Sis has it golden. Mom says when she was her age, she got raped by two brothers and aborted a child.

The chunk of bacon I ate is still stuck in my throat, a scratchy raft, the taste like an ashtray slurping itself.

I won't eat if Sis won't.

You should have some, I say, scooping up soupy eggs and two leather bacon strands onto another plate.

Sis looks at me with dumb doe eyes, faded denim−blue and sleepy. When I push the plate across the table, Sis screams and jumps up and screams and screams, body convulsing until I grab her plate and mine and flip the food into the trash basket under the sink.

When I come over to her, Sis stands rigid, her neck bent, looking like a light pole. She flinches when I touch her elbow but lets me guide her across the room and through the screen door until we're well past the trailer lot and sitting on the edge of a gravel pit, staring into the wide hollow that was once filled with sellable rubble.

Are you ashamed of me? Sis asks. Do I scare you?

Sometimes. Not ashamed, but, yeah, I get worried.

When Sis punches the ledge of dirt we're sitting on, a shelf of scorched soil shudders all the way down until it showers like fine powder, soundlessly on the ground.

It's just, I see things, Sis says. I hear things that other people don't.

I know.

It's not normal, but I see and hear them.

I know, I say. Remember, I'm your twin?

Sis flicks her head toward me as if just now comprehending that what I've said is true.

Yeah, twins, she says. I love that we're twins.

Me, too.

Sis grabs a rock and chucks it into the glare where it's swallowed by the sun, never ever landing.

Sometimes, Sis says, I want to kill myself.

Yeah.

The bacon said—

Stop, I say.

But—

But, for one thing, bacon never tells the truth.

What?

Just the other day, a piece of it told me I was hideous and way too skinny.

When Sis swivels her head, I'm afraid, but her eyes narrow and then she laughs.

You got one of the nicer pieces, she says.

I know, I say. But still, you really can't trust bacon. It's a motherfucking liar.

How Bacon Entered Our Consciousness (and My Stomach)

John Lane

As a connoisseur of food, I found myself returning to my favorite breakfast fare, bacon.

Bacon is a versatile piece of pork. It adapts itself well to many different meals, from an omelet's greasy side dish to a bacon, romaine lettuce and beefsteak tomato sandwich. According to www.fatsecret.com, one slice of cooked bacon equals forty–two calories with sixty–nine percent fat, twenty–nine percent protein and one percent carbohydrates.

According to a 2016 *Washington Post* article, bacon always had a home at the breakfast table. However, during the early part of the twentieth century, companies like Kellogg's and Post ran competing marketing campaigns that promoted the healthy benefits of pre–packaged cereals. Meatless options, like Corn Flakes and Grape Nuts, became increasingly popular. Recognizing the lack of interest in bacon, The Beech–Nut Packing Company, a pork producer, hired Mr. Edward Bernays, a public relations personality, to reacquaint the American public with the pork–cured meat. Mr. Edward Bernays was in contact with a certain doctor, and Mr. Bernays asked him about the necessity of a more sustainable breakfast. The doctor agreed. Later, the two reached out to about five thousand doctors to "confirm" their belief. The resulting "public opinion" saw bacon placed in a more positive light. The American public looked with favor on bacon and eggs as another breakfast choice. Even the phrase "bacon and eggs" became part of the American lexicon.

Based on data from the U.S. Census and Simmons National Consumer Survey, over eighteen million Americans consumed over five pounds of bacon each in 2019. However, as Americans have become more health conscious, different bacon varieties have been touted. Coconut, duck, elk, venison and turkey varieties have given Americans more freedom to couple the need for bacon with their lifestyle.

As a modern–day consumer who speaks with his wallet, I enjoy nothing less than a perfect slice of bacon. Bacon should be completely flat, cooked evenly to expose its golden–brown color. There should not be any burnt or white, fatty ends to dominate its texture. The taste should be a combination of sweet and salty. The result makes for a mouth–watering experience.

Enjoying bacon has created a lot of memories for me. I crawled on my grandmother's lap to smell the smoky aroma from the frying pan. I was mesmerized when the waitress at Denny's brought my Grand Slam order with two crisp slices. I bought my first jar of Baconnaise from the local grocery store. I stayed overnight at the Best Western Rockville and was rewarded with unlimited bacon for my breakfast. I attended every Pennsylvania Society of Public Accountants breakfast meeting that included bacon on the menu.

I learned one thing in my education of bacon. It is the ultimate comfort food for me.

Song of Bacon

Patti Cassidy

The bacon's smell wafts through the floorboards from the kitchen below.

My neighbors are frying a most enticing breakfast.

Bacon in their kitchen.

Bacon in my hall.

I myself have no bacon.

It torments me because I am haunted by the cries of pigs.

I won't buy it because of their pain and the methods of hog farmers.

But I feel it in my mouth and hallucinate the deep, rich, pink taste

From just breathing the fragrance

When the neighbors start to cook.

Quiet

Gwendolyn Joyce Mintz

Francine averts her eyes as her son yanks his boy from the booster seat, watches the milk from the upset cup spread across the table. She snatches the plate of bacon from the path of the white stream, places napkins in front of it, a paper dam to keep it contained. She ignores her son's booming anger and her grandson's shrieking fear. She wants to intervene. She got the help she needed; learned about other, better tools. Her son had glared at her when she tried, once, to share. His face set hard, he'd told her: Just be quiet. Like you were all those years Dad was beating my ass.

Praying for Bacon

Eve Rose

Once a year, my father and grandfather skipped dinner, left their wives, and raced 90 miles up the Long Island Expressway to spend the night in sin. For some reason, they took me with them.

Both prominent rabbis in New York, they loved to talk shop on the long drive: failed sermons, annoying Bar Mitzvah boys, the latest anti–Semitic hot spot. But as soon as we arrived, they stopped talking.

I don't recall the name of the restaurant, but I do remember the bordello–like décor – red leather booths, velvet curtains, gold–painted chairs too heavy for my little girl arms to pull out.

They would enter through a side door near the bar, ask for a table in the back corner and quickly place their order: Bacon–wrapped scallops and a pound of lobster. A trifecta of forbidden foods. Jewish law is unequivocal: Shellfish and pigs must never touch our lips.

During dinner, I'd fight to stay awake, not wanting to miss their cloak and dagger antics: my grandfather constantly pulling the brim of his fedora over his eyes; my father wearing his black horn–rimmed sunglasses INSIDE; the candle on the table the waiter was not allowed to light. The way they both shouted NO! when I asked to taste their meals. I knew we were doing something bad, but was not sure what.

Now I know. They'd picked the farthest, most obscure restaurant to eat bacon and lobster so they wouldn't get caught by their congregants. It was one thing for Mr. and Mrs. Goldberg to eat bacon on the down low. Another for the rabbi to do it.

Once the food arrived, they'd eat like they prayed: fast and intensely, breaking pace only to scan the restaurant for congregants. No dessert, no lingering at the lobster tank. If I wasn't done with my baked potato, too bad. Eat, pay, flee.

I'm not sure why they took me with them. Was I a bacon alibi? *"We're just showing her what not to eat,"* they might say if a congregant turned up. A bargaining chip with my mom? *"We'll take her if you let us go."* What mother doesn't want to get rid of a child for a few hours?

Maybe they sensed that one day I would betray the faith, declaring my atheism at 16 like I was coming out of the closet; marrying a non–Jew, and eating crispy rashers at every opportunity.

Even now, I feel defiant when I eat bacon. Bacon is the ultimate in unkosher. Like Voldemort in *Harry Potter*, some Jews will not even say the word aloud, calling it a davar acher (another thing). My mother wouldn't even buy me a stuffed animal pig. I'm sure a lobster or scallop toy would have been OK, though their living models were just as unkosher. There's just something about bacon.

I didn't understand the threat until I married. When my husband found out about my bacon–less life, it was too much for him to bear. He'd look at me as though I had grown up in a windowless bunker.

I started with a pork chop and then ham, practically spitting out both. At 36, the flavors were just too unfamiliar. I had yet to experience the bacon override, the love at first bite. Yes, like my forefathers, I too would break rules, risk my reputation, and drive hours in the night for this delight.

I'm not alone. Even the most religious Jews are seduced by the swine. In Israel, one restaurateur learned to make bacon from kosher lamb. Now, traditional, observant Jews flock to him for the simulated experience. *Forward* magazine talks of a "rogue rabbinic scholar" who claims that the prohibition on bacon was for high priests only. The rest of us schmucks need suffer no longer. There is even a "literary archive" called the *Pork Memoirs*, in which Jews write of their shared culinary trauma.

But seriously, why is bacon a sin? Why not celery or cabbage? It sure as hell ain't marketing. How can we possibly compete with Christians and their crackling?

Some ancients thought pigs were unclean and might spread disease. I've used this pseudo−science to justify kosher laws to non−Jewish friends, hoping to make my people look saner. I never tell them just how crazy it can get. One law says you can't eat a kosher animal if it looks like an unkosher one. (No cows with the jaw line of a pig!) There are more spiritual interpretations − deprivation shows devotion. Bacon or God? God or bacon? Ok, I get that.

I've decided it's religious buzz kill. From booty calls to bacon, most faiths look down on pleasure.

My father and grandfather are long gone so I can't ask them how often they cheated or how it made them feel. They stopped taking me to their swiney soirées when I turned 11, old enough to know what's what. I imagine they felt pretty guilty. Even with all my bacon bravado, it's not just my greasy fingers that still make me feel a little dirty sometimes.

Dissonance

Gertrude Walsh

Tom paused, his teeth deep into crusty bread, melting butter and crisp, salty bacon. The fifteen minutes of preparation, hot grill, flicking them just before the fat burned, him salivating. Bread spread ready for rashers, hot, that oozed butter through fresh cut sourdough slices. And then she started...

"Cognitive Dissonance... yes, that's it... here," she pointed to the definition on her phone. "It's '*having inconsistent thoughts, beliefs, attitudes, especially relating to behavioural decisions*', right? So how can you be a dog lover and eat bacon? How can you say you can't resist eating a pig's arse? It's hypocrisy, and your generation think you are capable of educating us?"

Saturday mornings evolved through years of nurturing her, lovingly first with warmed bottles of dairy–based formula, highchair moments of cheesy pasta, sandwiches with victuals diverse and exotic that built her mind and body strong.

He sighed, reluctant now to trash her newfound confidence, the power she gained going headlong to battle with an ageing army, her parents! Not just her parents but all of Tom's generation. The vile destroyers of planet Earth, with wasteful consumption, economic ruin, planet careering to climate extremes. He could see the rashers cooling, little blobs of fat congealing with butter and compressed bread where his fingers gripped lovingly the dream of Saturday morning. He eyed the glass of juice, the hot cup of tea and newspaper, distracting, full of the worries and woes real or imagined to occupy his mind for a few pleasant hours.

She munched her bowl of granola, berries from Morocco, soya milk from 'God knows where', the top sprinkled with almonds and walnuts. The nutritional feast and vast air miles occupied her mouth for moments enough for Tom to weigh up the situation. Thinking, 'Do I argue, or relent? It's unlikely I'll win, and to be fair, it's a good strong starting point. And, another positive is that at least her education has shown some benefits.'

"What do you **suggest I do, Emily?**" he kindly said.

He could feel a tension, the loss of a perfectly prepared, now wasted bacon−butty and the longing to end these pointless arguments that he knew he'd never win.

"Go Vegan, that simple."

Her blue eyes as clear and innocent as a baby, as hard and ruthless as a determined killer. And she could hold a stare, chewing, crunching all the while to perfect health and a life potentially ten decades long.

"Simple," he mused, slowly stated, and without her enthusiasm.

Tom pondered, he even placed a finger on his chin for effect. She might even think he was considering this as a future option.

Silently, he considered. 'I mean, isn't that what good parenting is about? You should listen to their well−formed arguments, consider their feelings, dance carefully so confidence isn't shattered but not so much that you patronise. There are all sorts of dangers now for young people that unwittingly were ignored in times past. She may be anxious, empathising with the sentient creatures we care for as pets. There could be lasting consequences her being the daughter of a trader in flesh, stigmatised within her society, isolated, shamed. What if she becomes a compulsive liar pretending to her friends that I never was a smoker, a drinker? That's off limits too!! I'm beginning to think that through her eyes my vices will make her portray my life as one of wild hedonism, reckless escapades, and I let it go, willingly. She may yet describe my follies, turn me to a hero of Rock and Roll proportions. So I am glad to have found a reason to relent. A simple sacrifice. I love *simple*.'

Measured now, he spoke.

"Simple, is it, Emily? I will give it further thought."

Many battles are worth conceding.

Tom pushed against his chair, lifting the small white plate, depositing with a thud his now abandoned dream into the brown, food waste bin. Grabbing Bruno's lead, he smiled.

"I think he needs a walk. I will consider, maybe, I do see your point, the dissonance thing, it's a big change for me, you know. I'm a creature of habit but I understand your concern."

Without even glancing up as the lead clipped around the ring on Bruno's collar, "Would you like to come too?"

Joe's Café has water bowls for dogs, traditional fry-up breakfast all day. Tom relished, scoffed even, and 40 minutes later was walking home again, thinking over her answer to his invitation:

"Not today," she'd said, her phone now occupying her with new Earth-saving ways.

La Diablesa Tocina

Paul Jauregui

Bacon!

  Tocino!

  Speck!

  Cig moch!

  Baaaaaaacon!

A word so important that it no longer means simply an item of food, cut from an animal.

Bringing home the bacon. You are the provider for our family, clan, society. You perform the most important role there is.

You saved my bacon. Were it not for your intervention I should have lost my life, my livelihood, a really great opportunity. I owe you an enormous debt of gratitude, which will be hard for me to repay.

I know Jews and Muslims who would turn pale and run away screaming if I waved a ham sandwich under their noses, and yet they eat bacon sarnies without blinking an eyelash. Ketchup and mustard are optional, but that pig meat cooked to near obliteration, such that it is a crispy beyond what generally constitutes an acceptable degree of hard and crunchy, is the essential item for an English breakfast.

Die—hard traditionalists will insist that even grilling it is a crime worthy of permanent banishment from the kitchen. It must be fried. And not in some namby–pamby Mediterranean oil, but fat. Lard. Add the grease. Pile it on. Clog those arteries. And it has to be in a flat circular pan on the hob. That arrangement maximises the aromatic emissions and causes the supreme amount of grief to those attempting to abstain.

Perfection.

There have always been three culinary aromas that have tickled my nostrils like some cartoon character. They are: fish and chips, coffee, and bacon frying. (Please see above regarding grilling.)

When I became a vegetarian, thirty–five years ago, two of my scent–related addictions were removed from the menu and became the 'no–nos'.

Or so I thought.

It was hard in the beginning. At first I was fine, but when I walked past a chip shop those cartoon fingers gripped my nose and dragged me in. But it was relatively easy to convince my feet to turn around and exit the emporium, my reasoning being that it was the devil inviting me in, and anyway, that stuff is deep–fried for three days and is going to kill me really quickly.

So that was one down, I congratulated myself, as I sniffed long and deep at the coffee jar.

But the bigger challenge still needed to be confronted.

I would wake in the morning to discover someone else in the house was cooking bacon, the smell rising to my bedroom. I knew that on the landing or in the bathroom the aroma would strengthen, and if I even considered going downstairs it would seize my whole being.

Should I stay in bed all day? No. I needed breakfast. I had to venture into the kitchen where the evil temptress awaited me.

And so I made it as close as possible without succumbing, then held my breath, ran into the kitchen and flung open all the windows, opened the cupboards and pulled out the coffee, removed the lid and put my nose over it; breathing in deeply.

It almost worked.

I relaxed and leaned back on the worktop, believing I had vanquished my demon. But as soon as I did, she gripped me. Taking me where I must not go.

She is the evil one. A harpy. La diablesa.

"Bacon, you are a wonderful servant but a dreadful and terrifying mistress."

She does not hear me or does not care. My anguish is what she desires.

But I shall be strong.

I must be strong.

I am strong.

No.

I am weak.

She takes me.

Yellow Delight

Andrew Sellors

What was his name? Baker? Bacon? Yeah Bacon. I start to piece him together again as I slither into the clarity of consciousness. Fuzzy names aren't enough to satisfy me though, and in the dark feel my way across his bed for something more tactile. I rapidly detect a void where there should be taut, smooth skin but instead only air absent of rhythmic breathing. I lay a palm on his pillow – cold. However, there is something, a piece of paper. I jolt into an upright position and scratch around for a table lamp or my phone – whatever will fight the dark – I can't find anything though. Sitting on the edge of the bed I'm disorientated by the mysterious relief of his living space. At that moment I crave light and its warm pastoral arm. I need it and need it now. I'm prepared to do anything to get that yellow delight.

The Full English

Lynda McMahon

A cooked Full English on the breakfast menu is a prerequisite for a satisfactory hotel stay. The yearning for bacon cannot be ignored nor gainsaid. When the urge is upon me I will not be dissuaded. It has to be the full works: bacon, sausage, eggs, beans, mushrooms, tomato and black pudding. Actually, I can do without the black pudding, which is one meat product too far, but there must be bacon. Fried not grilled. Please don't pretend it's healthy. I want fat and lots of it.

At home I have a slice of toast and a cup of tea because I can't face much first thing. When I check into a hotel which has, probably, been chosen on the basis of its breakfast menu, I become an iteration of the Incredible Hulk: a ravenous carnivore gripping my breakfast hardware like primitive tools ready to spear my prey. I enjoy every morsel because it's a rare treat, something I seldom consume at home out of respect for my husband's long–standing veganism. But if somebody else cooks it for me, it doesn't really count. Does it?

The Full English is the epitome of luxury consumed when there is the leisure to enjoy it. We might imagine that some version of this hearty breakfast has been around for a very long time and we would be right. As far back as the thirteenth century the lord of the manor prided himself on the quality and quantity of food he could offer friends and visitors for breakfast.

No bacon though, sadly, as it wasn't until the eighteenth century that curing bacon was discovered.

At this point in its history the Full English becomes charged by the class divide. The workers, on the land, filled up on bread and ale whilst the gentry tucked into what we begin to recognise as a cooked breakfast. As we watch televised versions of Jane Austen novels we marvel at the amount of food they shovel away: bread, meat, pies and fruit; and that's just for breakfast. The food is prepared for them below stairs and appears, miraculously, onto their over–laden table. The class divide is evident not only in the foods consumed but also in the manner of their preparation and consumption. By the time the Victorians were ensconced in their villas, the cooked breakfast became a means to ape the gentry; those who wander, languidly, down stairs expecting to see a side board groaning with food. Not just the Full English as we know it but also devilled kidneys, kippers and, sometimes, snipe and woodcock. By the nineteen twenties the staple fare of country house living was reinforced by dishes brought back from imperial rampages in other lands. For example, kedgeree and curried eggs. The cooked breakfast became a symbol of the leisured classes. Who had time for such elaborate food if they had to catch the early train to work? What they did have time for was a quick fry up of the basic elements of bacon, eggs and fried bread. By the nineteen fifties 50% of all adults began the day with a cooked breakfast.

So, where does the Full English I hanker after fit within this eighteenth century view of class and prosperity? Why do we who rarely attempt manual labour, still want to consume a 'big' breakfast? Along with the lure of juicy bacon it's the concept of luxury. Someone has to get up before us and provide this feast.

Discreetly. Whilst we shower, they do the cooking below stairs, or at least in the kitchen out of sight. We have our very own cook, for a short while at least, dedicated to our comfort and appetite. Like the gentry we descend gracefully to the hotel dining room wearing our polite morning smiles and nod benignly to our fellow guests as we are shown to our table and invited to peruse the menu before helping ourselves to juice, fruit and cereal from the buffet. I've stayed in places where they've offered dried apricots with vanilla and ginger, whole honeycomb, fresh baked bread and homemade jam. These all add to the sense of luxury, but they are not the main event.

Sometimes the menu description of the Full English is a very sad misnomer. When it arrives the mouth–watering anticipation is replaced by disappointment. On a very large plate is a very small amount of food: a tiny, dry, rasher of bacon, a flaccid egg, a thin sausage of very dubious provenance, two button mushrooms, half a small tomato and a miniscule ramekin of indifferent baked beans. By serving the beans in these pots the proprietor can get away with a dessert spoon full whilst looking elegant! This is a disgrace of a meal. As a guest I feel unloved, undervalued and duped. The promise was not fulfilled. I want to demand a refund but I am far too English, far too polite so I suffer in silence and vow to never darken their doorstep again.

The Full English should transport the consumer to another age but without the exploitation. For a time I want to pretend that I am Lady Smythe living a different life as long as breakfast lasts. I'll go back, happily, to being plain old Mrs Smith afterwards. The Full English is as much about what it represents as the food. We don't have time in our chaotic daily lives to grill, fry, scramble and toast the various components, so it really is a luxury. The very best Full English mimics the nineteen twenties house party: a buffet with huge, hinged tureens from which you help yourself, an 'all you can eat' of the best kind where the tureens are topped up when it looks like there might be a danger of supplies running out.

I don't want to go back to the life of upstairs/downstairs and all that suggests in its inequality. But playing for a while is jolly nice.

Six Degrees
of Entertainment

Rita Wilson

My savvy daughter and my clever niece have been urging me to open an Instagram account for over a year now. Each has in turn shown me cool things that you can do on Instagram: post stories and photos, see pictures and videos, like, comment and follow. I don't see where it's much different from Facebook. Isn't a "sticker" just a glorified emoji? How much difference can there be between two social media platforms owned by the same company? But, "If you want people to see your art, Mom," and, "If you want people to know about your book, Aunt Rita," you HAVE to get an Instagram account. So, I did, with some online tutoring from my daughter, because in the days of Social Distancing, that is the only way to do it. And now, it's just another thing to add to the growing amount of "screen time" I spend daily during this lockdown. Sometimes, I robotically scroll through paintings, sometimes I click on a video. I've connected with a few "friends" (mostly the ones I'm already friends with on Facebook), and I follow a few artists, and vice−versa. I'm annoyed with the same ads that annoy me on Facebook. I've been trying to figure out what I could possibly get out of an Instagram account, when I landed on a post by Kevin Bacon. *The* Kevin Bacon – the one who made me laugh in *Animal House*, captured my heart in *Footloose*, and mesmerized me in *Apollo 13*. Was he still around? I hadn't seen much of him in the past decade, but there he was in a video, a little scruffy, as we all are at this point – I guess even stars can't get to the salon. I clicked on the link and he came to life, with a Monday Blues playlist he shared on an old turntable to "lift us up." He played a song on a scratched Beatles Album, followed by the Beach Boys' *Little Deuce Coupe*, observing, "Who knew a song about a car could make so much money?" I began scrolling the Kevin Bacon videos. I watched his original, *No One Wants a Selfie Anymore*, entertained by the lamentation of the social distancing by former fans who would "rather stay healthy than get a picture with a star." I discovered that The Bacon Brothers have music, good music, on all the streaming sites (I'm listening to their *Americana* album right now). I laughed at Bacon's spoof of *Cuando Cuando,* which he sang, unabashedly, in black square rimmed glasses and a three– or four–days growth beard, accompanied by some sort of guitar or ukulele as his wife shook a box of Morton Salt for rhythm. It was the first time I'd laughed out loud in a few days.

If Instagram has brought me Kevin Bacon, I might as well keep it. For now, I'm waiting for tomorrow's post to pull me out of the Monday blues. And then, I guess I'll keep scrolling – who knows what else I might discover!

The Brooch

John Maskey

"What's this, a peace offering?" Joanne said as Mike slid the small box across the table.

He nodded.

"It's just a little something to say I'm sorry. Open it."

"Wow, it's gorgeous."

"It's the least I could do," he said, as he pinned the brooch to her lapel. "I'm sorry for the way I've behaved lately. It suits you."

"It's goes so well with my jacket. Why did you choose the bumble bee? Is it because I'm as sweet as honey?" Joanne's face hardened into a mock frown. "Or is it because I sting when angered?"

Mike laughed. "No, it's because I get a buzz out of you."

She groaned at his joke then blew him a kiss over the table.

"Whatever the reason," she said. "I love it. Thank you."

Mike sipped his coffee. The café was busy. Some jazz he couldn't identify was purring from the speakers. He didn't want to be overheard.

"It's nothing really," he said in a low voice. "I just wanted to say sorry for blowing up like that. I acted like an idiot. I'm so sorry."

Joanne leaned forward.

"As I told you the other night, there is nothing for you to get jealous about."

"I know, I know," said Mike. "And I'm sorry that I get so possessive. It's just that I've had my heart broken before. My marriage fell apart when my ex left me for someone else. And since I met you, well, I've been so happy but I get so worried that you'll meet someone else. And then I become frantic that this irrational jealousy will drive you away."

Joanne pushed her coffee cup aside and clasped his hand.

"Look, we all get a bit insecure at times. We've been together for what, three months? It's been great apart from a couple of bumps in the road. But I find it annoying and unhealthy when you demand to know where I've been all the time, or who I've seen, or who has called me. You have to stop this."

Mike nodded. His teeth clenched.

"We either have something to build on or we don't," said Joanne. "If we are going to grow as a couple then you must learn to trust me. Because without trust, there's nothing there."

He exhaled loudly and nodded.

"You're right. I'm sorry. I'll change. I promise you."

Joanne smiled and squeezed his hand.

She glanced at her watch.

"I've got to go back to work. Are you coming?"

She picked up her bag and stood up.

Mike shook his head. "No, I've ordered a bacon sandwich. I'll finish it and then head home."

Joanne leaned forward.

"Why don't you come round to mine tonight?" Her voice dropped to a whisper. "I'll cook and then I can thank you properly for this lovely brooch."

She gave him an exaggerated wink.

Mike grinned. "It's a deal. I'll be there at seven. With wine."

She blew him another kiss and headed for the door.

Mike was still smiling as he watched her cross the road.

When she disappeared around the corner he picked up his phone and clicked open the app he had downloaded earlier.

He could see the route Joanne was taking.

A camera was embedded in the brooch.

Taking Flight

Lisa Marie Lopez

"As soon as I see a bluebird, we can go," Alice told Jed.

They were sitting in the abandoned lot beside Big Dipper bowling alley, another warm summer day spread out before them like an uncharted map. Jed shrugged and continued working on his latest chalk art: an eagle, the size of a mountain. He hadn't worked on it since the day before. Yesterday, he and Alice sat in front of Vic's Antiques for nearly an hour, until Alice finally saw the Monarch butterfly she'd set out to see. "I don't get it," Jed said, rising up to stretch. "Yesterday we saw three bluebirds."

Alice laughed and patted the pavement beside her, an invitation for Jed to sit down. She had outgrown the thrills of collecting frogs at Millwood Pond and listening for the ice cream truck. These days, she'd much rather play around with new hairstyles, or hang out with Jed. Alice frowned when Jed ignored her invitation. Instead, he knelt back onto the pave—ment in front of the eagle, filling in its eyes with yellow chalk. Alice reached into her purse and pulled out the latest issue of *All About Me*, a teen magazine. No more than two pages in, she found herself sitting beside Jed, the magazine tucked back into her purse. She admired the eagle, but it was the auburn highlights in Jed's hair that captivated her most. She thought about what it would feel like to run her fingers through it, when she heard a woman's voice call out, "You kids need to leave. This area isn't meant for hanging out."

Alice turned around and saw a woman standing on the corner of the building, her face scrunched up with contempt. In her teal shirt, Alice saw she was an employee from the bowling alley.

Alice helped Jed collect his chalks and pack them into her purse. Then she gathered her hair into a ponytail, tying it up with a sparkly—purple rubber band. It was the same type of rubber band she saw on the sleek hair of the girls who graced the pages of *All About Me*. The back of her neck felt damp and she was glad Jed had brought along an extra Gatorade from home. They wandered to the other side of the lot and sat under a large tree. The warm, greasy aroma of bacon floated out from the diner across the street. Alice closed her eyes, inhaling it as if it were the most scrumptious thing she had ever smelled. Since discovering *All About Me*, Alice had refused to eat foods that weren't lean or complexion—friendly.

Jed sniffed the greasy bacon aroma, he too closing his eyes for a moment. A grin spread across his face. "Want to get a side of bacon from Nell's Diner? We can get it to go."

Alice shook her head, wishing bacon was one of the healthy foods raved about in her magazine. "I'm still trying to find that bluebird," she said. Glancing across the lot, she noticed the grouchy employee had gone. She nudged at Jed's sleeve and they sneaked back to their original spot. Near the drawing, a cat without a tail was prowling the pavement. Jed proceeded on with his eagle, filling in the head with white chalk. Alice settled beside him, waving her magazine towards her face. "I can't believe we start middle school next month," she said. "Do you think I'm going to fit in?" The cat pounced onto the drawing, pawing at the eagle's beak. Alice reached to pet the cat but it ran away from her. Jed turned to Alice with pleading eyes. "What about that? That's better than seeing a bluebird."

She whispered, "Yes, the cat counts," and stared into his eyes. Surprisingly, he didn't budge. Alice leaned in. His eyes were drowning in hers. She pressed her lips softly against his. He opened his mouth, just enough for her to show him a new side of life.

The eagle would lay on the sidewalk for the rest of the summer, unfinished. Only its wings were complete: dark−brown feathered and widespread, ready to take flight.

Beans

James FitzGibbon

One evening, we found his flat and just went right on in.

He looked round and said:

Hungry, man. Gotta get some milk and some beans. Love beans. You can do so much with 'em. Especially good on toast ... or with bacon or sausages. Not those cheap pink ones, the ones from the butcher's. Though I try to get the vegetarian ones these days. Not right that a living creature give up life just to please us, is it?

He turned round and looked at us.

Imagine it. Sorry, cow, you need to die so we can have sausages.

The cow, she says: "For Goodness sake, just bloody go vegetarian! I have children, my hobbies and pastimes. Not ready to give all that up ... For what? To lie beside some chips?"

Not right, *he said.*

Mind you, *he said conspiratorially.* What about them chickens? I tell yer: we owe a huge debt to chickens. Mark my words, *he said, wagging a dirty finger at us.* The great chicken in the Sky will see us at the Day of Reckoning ... with a bus conductor's machine that adds up. And say, "Erm ... let me see ... that's four thousand lives you've taken. Bloody kerCHING! How do you wish to atone?"

And he turned back to the TV.

So, I'm eating beans. That kinda stuff. Don't want to meet that big chicken, man. I tell yer: he's mean. And he means revenge. Some kind of retribution. And quite rightfully so. He's probably personally lost friends. And behind him are the fish, and pigs and sheep. And they'll point their trotters and hooves at you and hiss "Murderer."

He turned back and said: Yeah ... beware! You might just be having yer ham 'n' eggs and thinking nothing of it. But you're eating someone's dad ... Or brother.

So anyway, I went to get them beans, yeah. And I thought I'd get some milk. And some mushrooms. And that bread looked good – all crusty and smelling like Heaven. And, why not, a few bananas. Go well with milk and a teaspoon o' brown sugar. Oh yeah, I need some o' that too. And those fish fingers look good.

Well, you can imagine how full and heavy my shopping basket got, yeah? Anyway, I went up to the cashier and the till started bleeping. Bleep ... Bleep. And the cashier bloke, he was so straight–faced ... You know: no smiling. I thought I'd draw a smile on his face with his biro, yeah?

But, I tell yer, I didn't do anything. Just didn't look him in the eye. Tell you why. His eyes were cold, man. Like a dead fish's.

Anyway, when all that bleeping had finished, he said: "That's fourteen thirty–eight."

I smiled. I was trying to act normal. And looked him in the eye. There you go: those eyes! They were like the windows of an empty house. Yeah ... lots of shadows and nothing much else. Creepy, they were ... I don't mind telling you.

I looked in my jeans pockets: no money. I checked my jacket: nope, no money there either.

"Ha," I laughed, "just one moment, fine sir."

I tell yer: I could feel those bloody fishy eyes all over me. And they were getting narrower, like those guys in *The Good, the Bad and the Ugly* when they were going for a showdown at High Noon.

"Hmm," I said. "Seems like I've forgotten my money."

I gave an embarrassed gesture in the hope that this was all an unfortunate oversight on my behalf and not some dreadful malice aforethought, which Mr. Fisheyes might be thinking.

I said: "Let me take this bag home. Throw it in the fridge. It'll stop the fish fingers from going off. And I'll be back with the money."

Even as I said this, it sounded fishy ... fishy, yeah? Knew that My Shiny Shoes Fisheyes would not buy it. And sure enough:

"Sorry, mate. Can't let you do that. Shop policy states that any unpurchased goods cannot leave the premises. Bag stays here."

Then Fisheyes the bastard grinned and spat out: "Pull the other one, why don't you?"

As you can imagine, that got me well riled! So I said:

"Do you think I won't come back? Do you think I'm a common thief? Is that what you think?"

And I leaned closer to him. It was horrible to do, but that's what I did.

"Huh?" I said.

He said: "Look mate. All I'm saying is that you can't leave the shop with those goods. Understand what you like from that. No skin off my nose."

Then it struck me.

And he moved closer to us. And we moved closer to him.

This was a horrible person. There was horribleness oozing out of every pore of his horrible face! And I felt such dislike for him that I laughed, a short, sort of shocked laugh and said:

"Are you accusing me of attempting to steal from this shop?"

"Look, mate. Pay for the stuff you've bought. That's all. I'm not accusing you of anything." No grin this time, though.

I could have said "fine" and gone off to get the money, but the guy had annoyed me. No. More. He was kinda threatening me.

By this time, quite a queue had formed.

I said: "I don't like the way you speak to your customers. I want to speak to the manager."

"I am the manager. Please either pay for your shopping or come back with some money. Choice is up to you. But the bag is staying here ... Next, please."

So, I emptied the bag and left, saying: "Obviously Customer Service isn't the strong point of this shop."

I went home, got some money, and went to another shop. Not going to that shop again. Never again.

We asked: 'Did you get your beans?'

You know what? I was so flustered that I forgot. Had a cheese sandwich instead.

The Last Bacon Sandwich

Daniel O'Donovan

"I don't envy the cooks here," Molly said as she looked at the menu. "Look at this thing! It is almost a centimetre thick."

Samantha smiled from across the table. "It's nice to have choice. Besides, people come from all over the world to stay here and, given the location, they want to taste something really delicious on their last morning."

"Yes, but this is the breakfast menu."

"So you don't want to choose first thing in the morning?"

"My brain usually doesn't initialise properly until later in the day. Well, I know what I want."

"Me too."

They pulled out their phones and tapped their orders on the app.

"Thanks for suggesting this, Sam. It is better than my plan."

"What was that?"

"Staying in bed until my alarm beeped and then a rushed shower before meeting you in the lobby."

"You should probably savour the shower, too."

"They don't have showers on Mars?"

"Of course they do, but mostly we'll be limited to military and not Hollywood showers."

"So... get wet, soap up, and wash off?"

"Yep," Samantha said, sipping her water.

"Sounds like we'll be very smelly when we arrive."

"We've been through university, which I think, on the whole, has more smelly people."

"Good point," Molly said. "I do feel rather famished."

"Well, hopefully the food on the trip won't be too bad. It will be like eating microwave meals for a few months."

Molly nodded. "You have mentioned that. Hopefully the discoveries we're going to make on Mars will more than make up for any culinary shortcomings."

"Amen to that. And we might want to keep that out of our interviews."

"Yes," Molly said. "It would look a bit odd mentioning the food. You don't hear interviews with Howard Carter or Neil Armstrong complaining about the food!"

"No." Samantha sipped her drink and her stomach grumbled.

"Looks like I am not the only one who is hungry."

A waiter entered carrying their breakfasts. They smiled. This place still used actual people for waiting staff and not far cheaper robots. "Good morning, Ladies."

Molly beamed and blushed as she looked at the waiter. There was something so attractive about his Indonesian accent.

"And how are you today?"

"Excellent," Molly said. "And you?"

"Better for seeing you, Ma'am."

Molly turned a deeper shade of red.

"Here you go." He placed their plates on the table with robotic precision, bowed his head, and moved away.

"He likes you," Samantha said.

186

"Obviously." Molly smiled.

Samantha returned the smile as she took up her fork. She had chosen the nasi goreng served with shrimp and a fried egg. "Delicious," she said after only one forkful of the rice. Then she noticed Molly's breakfast. "A bacon sandwich!"

"What?" Molly was liberally applying brown sauce to the crispy bacon.

"You've come thousands of miles around the world and, instead of having something local, you have one of the most quintessentially British breakfast foods there is."

"Yep," Molly said. "Like you said, we're leaving the planet in four hours and won't get good food for a while." She bit into her sandwich. This was followed by almost orgasmic sounds of enjoyment. "Mmmh mmmhmmh aaggaGGh GhGhhhh. That was good. And more bites to come!"

"Would you like to be alone with the sandwich?"

"It's fine. I have seen you make out with Mio often enough."

"You're comparing my husband to a bacon sandwich?"

"Yep."

Samantha laughed. "This is pretty good, too."

"Good." Molly took another bite. She settled for smacking her lips this time. "I am going to miss you so much," she told the sandwich.

"Er, Molly," Samantha said looking at the menu.

"What?"

"It's not real bacon. It is turkey bacon."

Molly made another 'mmmhmmh' sound as she took another bite. She shrugged. "It's my last bacon sandwich. Close enough."

"Sounds like it," Samantha said.

Molly held up the other half of the sandwich. "Look at that. Almost two centimetres of bacon. It is crispy in all the right places and perfectly prepared. Soon all we'll get is reconstituted meat that won't even be in the same league as this."

"No, but we'll be on Mars."

"Yes," Molly said. "Which is why I am coming with you. It will be a great adventure. Now if you'll excuse me, I need to concentrate." She closed her eyes as she opened wide. "Mmmhmmh," she said. "Better than close enough. This is good food!"

Ketchup or brown sauce?

Cathie Aylmer

Taking a deep breath and exhaling slowly, Sarah found her smile and opened the door. The boys hustled in to the room, a whirlwind of teenage hormones and stale body odour.

"Miss, what we doing today?"

"He's in my seat!"

"Oi! How is it yours?"

"This is shit."

So, it was going to be one of those days, Sarah thought, as she strode back across the room, squeezing between desks and tucking in chairs. "Come on boys, break ended 5 minutes ago," she pointed out, handing out books and pens, whilst checking the register. "Are we ready to start?" Sarah paused and scanned the students' faces. "Look at that bold headline on the screen," she said, standing next to the projector. *"Being bullied?"* she read aloud. *"Just act less gay, advise teachers."*

Benny sniggered, he was fourteen going on four, "It says gay!" he exclaimed.

"*You're* gay!" someone else retorted.

Sarah couldn't be sure who had said it, was it Kye? It didn't matter – whoever had said it, the attention of the class was slipping away, whispered conversations were starting and she needed to act fast.

"A good starting point, Benny, in what way do you think they are using the word 'gay' in this headline? Do you think it's an article about attitudes towards homosexuality and gay people in schools or an example of inappropriate use of the word as a derogatory or insulting term?"

There was a loud click as the projector suddenly switched off and Sarah's heart sank. She tucked stray hair behind her ear as she pressed buttons and checked cables. A paperclip ricocheted off the wall behind her, landing by her feet. Frantically she poked at the keyboard; without the resources on screen the lesson was doomed.

"Thank you for waiting sensibly," Sarah called out from under the desk, wiggling another cable.

But the class were taking full advantage of the interruption, missiles flying between the desks — pencils, pens, balls of pap — the majority missing their mark and littering the floor; any that didn't were swiftly and aggressively returned. Sarah suddenly felt hot, tripping over a chair as she attempted to reach the projector buttons and another projectile flicked past her. She just hoped anything that hit her wasn't saliva−soaked. Stretching towards the ceiling her shirt came untucked and she felt a rubber bounce off her shoulder, sweat was starting to form in her armpits, forcing her to be grateful she hadn't even had a chance to take off her jacket. In a minute or two it would be total mayhem...

"Hello!"

Sarah turned and a wave of relief washed over her as she saw Pete stood in the doorway. Pete was her classroom assistant and in the few weeks since she'd started working at the school, he'd also been her admin support, emotional support and, well, frankly, anything else she had needed him to be.

"What do you need?" he asked quickly, looking around the room making eye contact with as many students as he could and identifying who the likely trouble-makers were. A pen lid skimmed past Pete's ear hitting the doorframe beside him. Benny looked at another boy, pointing.

"Could you..." Sarah trailed off as she waved a hand towards the chaos in the centre of the room, "I just need to..." ...and at that point the projector whirred back to life.

"Alright, boys, what's it to be: ketchup or brown sauce?" Pete asked, as he sat at the desk next to Kye in the middle of the class, his solid presence creating a barrier that halted the flow of objects across the room.

There was a sudden lull in the noise as the boys' puzzled faces turned towards Pete.

"Ketchup or brown sauce?" he repeated. "You're having a bacon sarnie, what are you putting on it?"

Benny answered first, "I put butter on mine, then ketchup."

"I like putting sausage and egg in mine," someone added, "*then* ketchup."

"Nah," argued another lad, "loads of brown sauce, got to be."

Soon a roomful of chairs edged towards the large table where Pete sat. Sliced bread or baps? White bread or brown? Soft or crusty? All had been debated — consensus had been reached: it didn't matter so long as it was white — and even Kye had grudgingly acknowledged, "It's better with brown sauce, innit?"

Sarah stood beside the projector screen, her pulse slowing and her smile returned. The only sign of the disruption was a scattering of spit balls and stationery on the floor.

"What are we doing today then, Miss?" Pete asked, winking.

"We are looking at opinions in articles, but I think you've just cracked it for us." Sarah replied. "It seems we all have an opinion about our bacon butties! So that's what we'll write about."

Books were opened and pens were picked up; frowning with concentration the class hunched over their books scribbling down their opinions. Sarah's thoughts drifted to lunch time, her BLT sandwich, and the coffee she definitely owed Pete.

Bacon Sandwich

AJ Fowler

It is around month eleven that the dreams start. Flashes and fragments, coming back to me when I wake. Subconscious screams of rebellion that leave a salty taste in my mouth and weaken my resolve. Night after night I am haunted by a forbidden lust of bacon. And cravings for bacon sandwiches specifically. Crispy rashers tucked in between slices of squishy bread with generous helpings of melting butter. I am a purist, there is no sticky ketchup or acidic brown sauce to sully the taste, just bacon and buttery bread. And this is what my life has become, whole dreams of bacon. Frying the bacon, watching it crisp and waking just as my teeth are about to sink into the soft bread for that first salty bite. Sometimes when I wake, the smell of bacon fills the air, and I wonder how much longer I can hold out.

Nocturnal

Alex Reece Abbott

For Arthur T. Tranzsistah 7.10.1958 – 2.11.1993

Miss Diana Ross scans the street, then hitches up her frock. With a grunt, she takes a long, slow slash in the gutter, maintaining her cat–walk posture.

Girl's got her pride.

Miss Ross straightens her hem and struts on down icy Lambton Quay, one black, size eleven patent stillie dangling from her pinkie finger. Takes more than a snapped heel to derail this soul train.

Four a.m. and a half hour hike from the abandoned warehouse that she shares with her outlaw mates, she's still pure seventies disco diva. Falsies aligned, sparkling black acrylics unchipped, killer cheekbones skillfully highlighted with blusher. Her almond brown eyes are amped with cosmetics and chemicals.

Usually smoother than a billiard ball, tonight her beautiful bald head is crowned with a froth of jet curls. Her metallic off–the–shoulder sheath dress showcases slender arms and smooth latte skin. Long, toned, hairless legs flash when the leopard–skin side–slit gapes. Real men don't do winter.

The greasy, bacon–scented air calls to her. Being a fabulous legend is hungry work. It's risky, but she'd break a nail for a brekkie burger. She totters towards the Pie Cart, working her hit—list, magenta highlights trembling as she strikes that pose.

Nocturnal and spectacular, it's hard not to become a target. Under the cool sodium street—lights, blue—bubble wasps cruise the early morning revellers, keen to attack their quota and earn their stripes.

Miss Ross tosses her head and her diamante—ed lobes glint in the approaching headlights.

The patrol car pulls over.

Her thick lashes fluttering like ebony moths landing on her kohl—lined lids, Miss Ross hums one of her hits to fend off any buzzkill. In the middle of a chain reaction alright.

C'mon, get in, Arthur.

A battered hoon—packed Falcon is belting up the Quay, closing in.

Her eyes widen with attitude, fuchsia lips pout then part, revealing a whiter—than—white smile. Yessss...*Of—ficer.*

Raising her unstubbled chin in casual acknowledgement, she selects the lesser evil.

Home please, purrs Miss Ross.

Little Pigs

Ann Liska

Jon's mother stared at the FedEx package with its strange return address and weird stamps.

"Nobody's hiring here, Mom. It's called the Great Recession." Jon unzipped the packet.

The Superior Technical University had sent a DVD, along with his e—tickets, which made it all seem real.

Jon's mother, Marcy, was an anxious person. When Lauren broke off the engagement, she took it harder than Jon did. And now her only child was going to work seven thousand miles away.

The DVD showed a panoramic view of a waterfront. People riding bikes. Fishermen casting lines from a concrete bridge. A family picnicking under a gazebo. This cut to an interior view of an office, men in long white garments, a black—veiled woman answering phones.

"Emiratis wear the national dress. Expatriates may wear modest business casual attire. Islam is the official religion. However, the UAE is a tolerant country. Christianity may be freely practiced." A brief shot of a church followed.

Next, a picture of what looked like a social gathering. Expats and locals drinking coffee out of tiny cups. A lavish food buffet. Everybody sitting on floor cushions.

"We are a hospitable, social people who value family and community."

"You will receive a comprehensive orientation once you arrive," the narrator concluded.

Along with the appealing images, there were warnings about alcohol and pork.

"Non–Muslims may be issued an alcohol license for home consumption. Pork is also available to non–Muslims. Do not consume any pork product in public or refer to pigs in conversation. Even a picture of a pig is offensive."

Jon thought about a book he'd loved as a young child. The book had buttons you could push, and little songs would play: the house of straw, of sticks, of bricks.

But really, who would bother to pack pictures of pigs?

People at church were confused about his new job. They knew about the Persian Gulf, Iran, Iraq. Some had even heard of Dubai. He was either brave or foolhardy, depending on one's point of view. Various things got back to him: he was breaking his mother's heart. He had never got over Lauren.

"I'm going there to work. To earn money," he said. "It's as simple as that."

At brunch Jon ordered extra bacon.

"You've never been that fond of bacon," Marcy commented.

Jon laughed. "It's the thought of being deprived of it," he said.

At the airport, his parents insisted on coming inside. He felt a pang as he waved good–bye from the security check lane.

At 18:00 exactly, he was in line for the Lufthansa flight that would take him to Frankfurt and then on to Abu Dhabi.

197

★

At the Hilton on his first UAE morning, he ordered a side of beef bacon. It was salty enough, but tough, tasteless. He never ate it again.

At school he was busy with the learning curve. His boss, a skinny Emirati man, was patient. Ramadan began, and the workday was shortened. Non–Muslims could eat lunch if they hid their food. Jon craved water, which wasn't allowed in public before sunset, no matter the weather.

Every weekend he was invited to parties, brunches, "leaving–dos."

He took the advice of seasoned expats – don't return home for at least six months. His parents were crushed.

"Why?" his father asked.

"It's too hard to get back on the plane. You need more distance," Jon said.

He knew they didn't understand.

"Hey, there's a ladies' night every Thursday on Yas Island," his co–worker Brian said. "Great place to meet birds. I mean, women."

"I'm familiar with the vernacular," Jon said.

"Blokes got to pay, but still, it's a good deal," Brian said.

On Thursday night Jon and Brian joined the line of taxis going to the island. Most were filled with women. "Birds!" Brian crowed.

Their second Thursday, he met Joanna.

"You're no fun anymore. Always with your bird," Brian grumbled in the break room.

Ramadan over, the room now smelled of curries and biryanis.

"Joanna's great, you have to admit," Jon said.

"Yeah. Too good for you," Brian answered.

Joanna was British. Jon loved her accent, her beauty, everything about her. Lauren receded in his memory, like a person from another life.

"You should join my church. St. Andrew's," Joanna said. For a second Jon wondered what his mother would say, but after all, church was church.

Cohabitation remains illegal in the UAE, although like everywhere else in the world, it does happen. For the time being, Jon and Joanna kept their own flats.

On Saturdays they went grocery shopping. They entered the area behind the sliding doors where the pork products were stocked. Besides the obvious things there were others: marshmallows, Pop-Tarts. Jon bought the pre-cooked bacon. Less messy, and the smell of it cooking less likely to offend the neighbors.

People are employed to make sure that all pork products entering the country go through the proper process. Even pet foods.

At Christmas they flew to the U.S., where they got engaged on New Year's Eve. Peter and Marcy came to Abu Dhabi for the wedding. Despite Marcy's trepidation, both of Jon's parents loved the UAE.

In 2016, Joanna got pregnant, and they decided it was time to leave. Marcy and Peter were scouting properties for them, and Jon was applying for jobs.

At the welcome—back brunch given by his parents, Jon piled his plate with pancakes, mini quiches, fruit, and a generous helping of crisp bacon.

"Hey, Mom," he said. "Do you still have that Three Little Pigs book?"

Marcy laughed. "Whatever made you think of that?"

"I dunno, I thought it would be nice to have for the baby."

His mother went upstairs and rummaged in the stockpile of stuff she'd saved for grandchildren.

Marcy handed Jon the book. It was in good shape, considering. "I put in new batteries," she said.

Jon opened the book and pressed the button on the first page. "I build my house of straw…" sang the first little pig.

Rash

Tim Jarvis

Marvin had bitten his nails down to the skin. His knees bounced with nerves and he tried to fill his head with the songs of Lionel Richie for distraction. He was on the second verse of *Dancing on the Ceiling* when his turn came around, right after the widower Valerie Lipsauce. He shot to his feet and introduced himself. "Hello, my name is Marvin Toothman and I'm a bacon addict." And for the first time in a long time, he felt human again.

It's hard being a bacon addict. Even harder being one in Texas. Marvin always thought that bacon was the duct tape of food. It wrapped around everything. If any dish needed a little fixing, they wrapped the damn thing in bacon. Chicken wrapped in bacon, eggs, peppers, they even had bacon condoms. It was called a Texas Twinkie. Everywhere he looked he could see bacon. And every morning he could smell it. Even when he tried to sleep at night, the distant crickets sounded like sizzling. Signing up to Bacon Anonymous was a real lifesaver. He saw their flyer on the town notice board a week ago. 'Bacon Anonymous. Shakin' the bacon'. They held meetings every Tuesday at the old chapel on Chesterton Avenue. And Marvin thought it was high time he took control. He knew he'd have to ween himself off in the coming weeks. Moving onto ham for a while to help his body adjust. It's the methadone to bacon they say. Sure, the road ahead was rough, but he was ready to be squeaky clean if you excuse the pun.

"Hello Marvin," the circle made up of the town's misfits all replied in unison. He smiled and continued. "I've been one week clean now. I can't tell you what it means to me to be here. To have found this support group." They smiled warmly and polite. Marvin felt like he'd finally been invited to the cool kids' party.

"So, why are you here, Marvin?" came the therapeutic voice of Chloe Longhorn.

Marvin took a deep breath, blinking to hold in the tears and continued. "Well. Like all of you, I've struggled every day with this. I can't seem to think about anything else. I'm in a cycle of shame and guilt. Powerless. I don't even know what day it is. I'm struggling to shake it. You know, I'm sure y'all the same too."

Like a church congregation, the people nodded in agreement. Some even let out a "ahmmm yes."

Marvin clenched his fists and continued. "I've done some bad things. Sometimes I look on the internet at things I shouldn't. I have a folder on my desktop, full of GIFs of bacon sizzling in a pan. All kinds too. Streaky, smoked, unsmoked. But it wasn't enough, you know. So, I moved onto the harder stuff. The Danish stuff. One night I snorted crushed bacon potato chips. It made me sneeze for three hours."

An older lady leaned in closer and screwed up her face: she was sure she hadn't heard it correctly.

"Two weeks ago, I was so low, at Lucky's Diner, I paid a truck driver to suck his Texas Twinkie. Just to get a taste again. He's called Rusty. A really polite man. He texts me some— times." The old lady now knew exactly what she heard. Her hands darted to and fro as she mimicked the sign of the cross. Some people just glared with wide eyes and wide mouths. Others pretended to be noticing something on the floor tiles. But like watching a dog chase its own tail, they didn't want to stop him either.

Marvin took a handkerchief from his back pocket and blew into it, sounding like a trawler coming into harbour. Fighting the tears again, he persevered. "Sometimes, on a weekend, I like to hide in the trees at the park during barbecue time...and watch people eating brisket and bacon. I lick my lips and imagine it's me."

"Marvin?" Chloe tried to interrupt this tail chasing. But Marvin was on a roll. It was cathartic now.

"Just last Thursday I sneaked out in the middle of the night to Harry Pickle's farm. I...I...just wanted to listen to the pigs. To be close to them. I found a baby one. A piglet. I played with it for thirty-seven minutes. Once it got used to me, it let me lick his belly. I licked his belly."

"Marvin?!" Chloe insisted.

It wasn't enough to stop him. "I think I like vaginas because they remind me of bacon. Not because they're vaginas."

Marvin stood up, blubbering. His face shiny with sweat, like a ham that's been wrapped up too long.

Chloe Longhorn stood up and stamped her feet like a kindergarten teacher trying to restore order.

"For God's sake, Mr. Toothman. I think you're in the wrong place. You want Bacon Anonymous. This is *Cupcakes*. Bacon is Tuesdays. Today is Wednesday. Just...get out!" she screamed.

Marvin shoved his hands in his pocket and quick–stepped out of the circle. Out of the church and out onto the street. He was a mixed grill of emotions, embarrassed, annoyed, relieved. This relief was short–lived as he realised he would have to do it all again tomorrow.

Like most times of stress, Marvin turned to food. He walked into Freddy's Diner, bought today's cupcake and sat in a booth by the window ready to devour it. Bettie, the waitress joined Marvin at his tableside and poured him a fresh coffee slowly with one hand, placing the other on Marvin's shoulder to offer comfort. "Didn't peg you for a cupcake man, Marvin," she teased.

"Cupcakes are for pussies!" he exclaimed, shoving the whole thing in until there was nothing left but the paper wrapper.

She rubbed his back and proudly said, "Well, I made that batch just this morning. It's got bacon and maple syrup sprinkles, your favorite."

Shit.

The Butcher

Michael Cieslak

Carefully.

Carefully.

Damn.

The knife slips and the blade slips along the belly. I drop the meat. A gray blur flies out of nowhere and snaps it up before it even hits the ground.

Part of me knows that this was going to happen, but that weird optimistic part of me grabs for it anyway. There was no way I would be able to save the sliver. It's gone with a slurp and the snap of canine jaws. Mitzie is gone before I can yell at her, but why would I yell at her? She wasn't the one who dropped the precious meat.

I return to the belly, frowning at the mess I've made. So far I have managed to pull off three perfect strips. All the rest are either mangled or misshapen. I am about to start cutting again when a shrill voice almost makes me drop my knife.

"How is it coming in there? Are you just about done dinking around?"

"Still working," I call back.

"Are you serious? We've already got the arms and legs trimmed in here. The hands and feet are boiling for stock and Grandma's filleted out the cheeks, tongue, and lips. We'd like to get in there and get the sweet meats, if you could get a move on."

I sigh, staring off at the pile of clothes in the corner. I'll need to throw those in the fire at some point today. I wipe my hands on the apron, pick up the knife, and go back to work on the body in front of me.

I really miss real bacon.

The Days of Bacon

Leah Holbrook Sackett

Starting in her 20s and into her married years, Miriam was a vegetarian. It wasn't always so. Rewind the clock, and find her wobbling in the unsteady gait of a two–year–old, down the little garden path between the houses. She's sniffing the neighbor's lush bloom of peonies with the full thrust of her chubby face; meanwhile, her Bubbe walks behind her, carrying a small plate of Bubbe's very best china topped with tender, crispy bacon for her highness in Pampers. Grandparents are notorious for spoiling their grandchildren, but no one had any idea it would go this far.

Then came the gluttonous adolescence. Miriam demanded bacon at every meal. Bubbe could smell the forbidden scent of bacon on her hands and in Miriam's hair. It was impossible to clean that bacon grease away in time for shul.

Finally, Miriam said goodbye to bacon when she met Abe. The stress, the smell eventually faded for Bubbe and Miriam. Years and children, bar mitzvahs and bat mitzvahs roll by until Abe passed early in his 50s. At the funeral, Bubbe thought she detected a whiff of bacon and said a prayer.

Miriam, like anyone, did not know how to grieve. She had the support and comfort of mourning from her and Abe's congregation. She tore her clothing and covered the mirrors, but she lacked the depth of surrender required to let Abe go.

Miriam needed to fill the gap left in her life. She was still sitting Shiva, but her body yearned for the consolation of a man. Miriam set boundaries to Shiva and stepped outside the community to Abe's long–time gentile friend, Andy.

At four in the morning, Miriam woke to the smell of bacon. It hailed back to her youth, and it diminished Miriam's grief just enough.

"Are you making breakfast?" she called as she rose from the bed.

"Don't come in here. I'm making you breakfast in bed."

Miriam slid back between the sheets. She pulled the flat paisley sheet up and tucked it tightly around her breasts to give them a little support, coverage, or something. The thick smell of sizzling bacon filled the room. Andy returned with a plate piled high with bacon and two Blood Marys balanced on a tray. The grease was on their lips and fingers, slowly covering every inch of skin with salt and fat. Miriam was a mess, and she loved it.

Bacon Culture

Jonnie Guernsey

I was cautioned against moving to this city just south of Milwaukee. *There's no culture*, my friends warned in ominous tones. No beer gardens, no good restaurants, not one theater. No museums, no concerts and probably no artists. Nothing. Never mind that I'm only seven miles from the Theater District, the Milwaukee Art Museum and The Riverwalk. Not to mention that trendy foodie hotspots and coffee shops dot every neighborhood northward between here and our shining downtown.

Atop this cultural concern, my friends pointed out that I am a liberal – a left wing pinko commie hippie remnant of the '60s. I was moving into unknown political territory where the very yard signs I display could result in shunning akin to the Salem Witch Trials.

"Look about you," one friend dramatically intoned. "Everything the light touches, that is Milwaukee. The shadowy place beyond our borders is Cudahy. You must not go there, Simba."

Ignoring their misgivings, I found a small stone house on the shore of Lake Michigan, in a county park strung along the "Emerald Necklace" wisely set aside by Milwaukee's socialist founders. Not only is it a stunningly beautiful location, but I am safely positioned in the Great Lakes Region, where water supplies will not be scarce should climate change continue unchecked in my lifetime. Or at least until You—Know—Who is out of office.

In other words, I'm sitting pretty. *But what the heck does this have to do with bacon*, you may well ask. It turns out that bacon is woven into the very fabric of our little city.

My understanding of this fact began to dawn as I sat on the patio one morning of the first week I lived in my new house. Out of nowhere, the distinct aroma of bacon wafted my way. It didn't take long for me to scramble into the car and head to a restaurant (in the trendy northern region) for breakfast with a side of bacon.

Next, it happened at the library. I stepped out into the parking lot and was overcome by a craving for a BLT. I hit the road for that other neighborhood to my north and indulged.

Soon after, while riding my bike through the park, trees all around, waves lapping the shore, seagulls screeching overhead, I yet again found myself salivating over that enticing scent, and pedaled my way – you guessed it – north in search of a bacon fix.

I need to mention at this point that: a) I don't eat meat in general, and b) I never cook bacon. Too messy. I believe in animal rights, and environmental protection, and not stock—piling toilet paper during a crisis so nobody 'goes' without. Still, living in Cudahy had somehow dissolved my willpower to avoid those strips of salty, fried, savory pork.

Who could be cooking all that bacon? Is every chef in every kitchen in the city constantly standing over a pan of sizzling bacon?

No. There is a perfectly logical explanation.

You see, the city is named after this guy, Patrick Cudahy. There's a statue of him in the local park that people frequently adorn with an empty can of Pabst. He pretty much built the town up from scratch, setting up shop here in the early 1900s. Soon people came to work in his production plant. Houses went up, and families became fiercely dedicated to living here for decades. In fact, the city motto is "Generations of Pride." This generation thing comes in handy. If I – a newcomer – need a plumber, or an electrician, or a tree–trimmer, all I have to do is ask, and somebody's high school sweetheart (to whom they may or may not be married), or cousin, or a kid they knew since second grade will arrive and skillfully take care of business. People look out for each other. All because of bacon.

That's right. Bacon. I live in a city founded on bacon.

Over the years, the Patrick Cudahy Company grew until they were producing tons and tons of bacon, shipped all over the country. You can find packages of Sweet Applewood bacon in your local grocery, made right here on Sweet Applewood Lane.

Bacon brings on what I was told was *the* social event of the city, not to be missed. Every summer, the local Lion's Club hosts the Sweet Applewood Festival. I tried joining the fun that first summer I lived here. People stood huddled in groups with – you guessed it – their high school friends, arms around their high school sweethearts (who they may or may not be married to), drinking Pabst to very loud rock bands blasting hits from the '70s and '80s. I stood on the sidelines, smiling like you do when you're the girl waiting to be asked to dance. This did not bode well in the Culture Department.

Luckily, that's not all Cudahy has to offer. We have our occasional concerts in the park. The traveling beer garden (yes, that's a thing in Milwaukee) stops here sometimes. Then the bronze Mr. Cudahy sports a plastic Sprecher Beer bottle, and we all carry our pint glasses and lawn chairs down the street to hang out with the neighbors. You don't get to do that in just any old town. Geologists and astronomers give fabulous tours on our bluffs. Birders flock to the region with their binoculars, giant zoom lenses and those vests with all the pockets they wear. Plus this is a hotbed for that geocaching Pokemon crowd. Let me tell you, just watching those birders and geocachers provides endless hours of fun. We recently added an art gallery, and a trendy coffee shop keeps promising to open soon. No one has shunned me when I plaster my yard with a line of signs supporting liberals running for election.

So, I'm doing fine here in Cudahy. There's culture, sort of. Not bedazzling, but still. I've even learned to resist the call of bacon. Most days.

Pie

Nod Ghosh

Tuesday morning, and I'm not speaking to my wife.

I'd rather not talk to anyone, but I have to call Frank to say I'm not going to the office.

"How long will you be off?" he asks.

"Don't know," I reply.

"Trust it won't be too long." He emphasises *trust*.

My boss knows I'm faking it. Probably heard me swear yesterday, minutes before I told him I was going home with a headache. It was just after I'd read Colin's email.

Jenny pokes her head into the spare room before leaving for her shift.

"I've made chocolate cake," she says. The aroma wafts in. "And there's steak pie." I shake my head and push the door. Our hands almost touch. She's still wearing her wedding ring.

"Suit yourself." Jenny's muffled voice barely penetrates the closed door. I turn the volume up. The documentary I'm watching is about ghosts, but ghosts can't mask my disgust.

Sean Clayton, Colin had said.

Of all the people, Jenny, why Sean?

Yesterday, I'd thanked Colin for his email, but wondered why he hadn't told me in person. Why send a photo when his office is ten metres away?

Sean Clayton. Saturday. That's all he wrote.

The picture showed a man's arm around Jenny. Their blurred faces were touching, her eyes closed, subdued light, people brushing against them. My wife had told me she was working an extra shift on Saturday night.

Colin always said Jenny was trouble, that I shouldn't have married her. He said she wasn't good enough for me.

I love my wife. And she cooks like an angel. Even Colin greedily consumes whatever she serves when he comes over for a feed.

When I came home early from work yesterday, there was a cottage pie on the table, peas and carrots too. Jenny often has my dinner ready before she leaves for her evening shift at the hospital.

"I'm moving into the spare room," I'd announced.

"Why?"

I hadn't replied.

Jenny's cottage pie is legendary, but I left it alone.

After she'd gone, I went out. The supermarket is quiet on Monday evenings. I bought crackers, cereal bars and several packs of noodles. I can look after myself.

Back home, I washed my face in the guest bedroom.

Sean Clayton.

Did she think I wouldn't find out? I retrieved an old electric kettle from the cupboard where we keep things that are breaking but too good to throw out. The cord is frayed. Grabbing crockery from the kitchen, I went to our bedroom for underpants, shirts and trousers. I took my razor and toothbrush from our bathroom and a pack of yellowing playing cards from the sideboard. I was settled in the guest bedroom before Jenny returned.

Though I'd eaten three cereal bars, I was hungry, so I poured boiling water over a block of noodles. While they soaked, I dealt cards for solitaire. I willed myself to pick a Queen in the first five moves. If that happened, I'd wake up, and this whole thing would have been a dream. I'd have my wife back. Sean would simply be a non-entity I worked with.

It was Colin who told me Sean had given Frank the 'anonymous' tipoff that led to my demotion. Now I don't even have an expense account to fiddle anymore.

The fourth card was a jack, the first picture card. The fifth card was the three of hearts. Two minutes later the noodles were still cardboard stiff. How long did they take? I read the instructions to discover they actually needed cooking. I decided I'd buy a microwave oven on Tuesday.

The documentary finishes as Jenny pulls her car out of the garage. I venture into the kitchen and encounter a chocolaty richness, though there is no sign of any cake. I'll buy myself cake after I pick the oven up.

When I return, the wholesome smell of Jenny's steak pie is still in the air. I've bought baked beans but forgotten the bread.

Crackers aren't as good, but I congratulate myself on my self–sufficiency.

"We have to talk," Jenny says on Wednesday.

I say nothing.

"I'm making butter chicken," she says. "Help yourself while I'm at work."

On Thursday it's fish pie. I love fish pie.

On Friday the house is filled with the scent of roast lamb.

On Saturday, I have to buy more noodles and cereal bars.

"There's lasagne," Jenny says as I leave. I ignore her and drive to the hills before shopping. You can see the whole city from here. Maybe I'll return to work on Monday. Frank's been bugging me.

On Sunday, Jenny taps on my door. She says they're short at work. She has to go in. More likely she's seeing Sean Clayton. She's left rich onion soup in a pan.

"I'm dying here," Frank says on Monday. "Can you cover Colin's client list when you've finished the accounts? Oh and there's Sean's audit report to — "

I can't take anymore, so I invent another headache.

When I return home, a meaty wood—smoke scent makes my mouth water. The house is silent, yet I sense a presence. A bacon and egg pie sits on the table. I lift it to my nose and inhale.

That's when I hear Jenny giggle. There's another voice. Creeping up the stairs, it doesn't take long to deduce what's happening. The rich scent of bacon screams to me. Just one bite before I confront them. Down in the kitchen, I attack the pie with my hands. No plate. No cutlery. After a week of noodles and beans, I'm ready for this. Every mouthful is a victory. Every morsel I devour is less for them.

The patter of Jenny's feet is followed by a man's steady footfall.

"You're home!" she gasps, pulling her dressing gown closed.

I bite into the last piece of pie, so satisfied that the shock of seeing Colin, rather than Sean, behind her barely registers.

But by then, the pie is gone.

Leaves of Bacon

Matt Potter

"This is really fucked," he said.

We were standing in *Religion, History of.*

I looked left and then right and for two seconds cocked my head, listening for footsteps or a book sliding off a shelf in the rows either side of us, or a giggle or breathing.

Then I grabbed a book at eye—level and slid it off the shelf.

Bryce shook his head.

I opened the book, reached into my pocket, pulled out a rasher of bacon and smoothed it across page 57. Then I snapped the book shut.

"It makes the book lumpy and it smells."

"It's a musty library," I said.

"I don't want you doing this, Jeffrey." He reached across to snatch it away but I clutched the book to my chest and hugged it close. "You know I could wrestle you for it," he said.

I sighed.

"And you'd enjoy it, too." Bryce breathed out and his fringe fluttered against his tanned forehead.

He looked so pained and so sweet! Lord, how had we got into this mess?!

Stupid question — I knew how! I was bored one day and found God and now I had to turn away from my sinful relationship with Bryce (with our gymnastic sex life and two cats) and find true love with a woman, the way God intends.

All I had to do was fall in love with the right woman. And then commit to her. And bathe in God's love. Just as all the guidebooks I'd read instructed.

Yes, I'd picked the woman, but …

Well, that's where the bacon came in.

"Bacon?!" Bryce hissed. "You fucking hate bacon!"

"I know, I know," I whispered, arms relaxing around the book. "It's too fatty and too salty. But it's God's will."

It was all planned: slip the bacon inside the book and pretend it was a gift.

"And Beatrice will probably love it," I said. "Who wouldn't love getting free bacon inside a book?" I flipped the book over and traced a finger along the gold embossed lettering on the spine. "Inside *The Jews of Moslem Spain, Volumes 2 and 3* by Eliyahu Ashtor?" I read aloud.

Bryce threw his hands in the air. "Her name is Heather, Jeffrey. *Heather.*" He thrust his hands onto his hips, stuck out his chin and bared his teeth. Then said, "It says *Heather* on her badge. Not *Beatrice.* But hey, what would I know?!"

I so wanted to place the copy of *The Jews of Moslem Spain, Volumes 2 and 3* by Eliyahu Ashtor with the rasher of bacon on page 57 back on the shelf, wrap my arms around Bryce's shoulders, hug him close and whisper in his ear, "It's okay, sweetie. Everything will be alright."

But it wouldn't. Because in our heightened state of tension, as we pulled closer and tighter and our bodies melted into each other, hard–ons would spring forth and we'd want to do something with them right now. In *Religion, History of.*

And I wasn't there to expend a boner. I was there to hand Beatrice, the way–too–skinny library assistant, a book with bacon inside it, as I slipped past the checkout desk on my way out. And to come back tomorrow and the next day and repeat. Until she remembered me. And gained some womanly curves from eating all that bacon.

I mean Heather.

(If I have to fuck a woman she has to have the whole package: hips, tits, the complete jiggle. Otherwise, there's no point, I may as well ...

I looked at the floor.

... I may as well fuck a man.

Well, that's where the bacon came in.)

Bryce flashed his doe (or buck) eyes at me. His hand slid along a shelf toward me and soon he stood straight up, right in front of me. His breath tasted warm on my lips.

"How many thousands of bacon strips do you think will turn Heather into the kind of voluptuous woman you might be able to shoehorn your cock into?" he whispered. "And also," he added, "what if she's vegan?"

"That's really distasteful, Bryce. You should show Beatrice some – I mean Heather – some respect. She's not just a piece of meat." And I opened the book again, whipped out the bacon rasher, flipped further into the book and smoothed the bacon across page 275.

Then snapped the book shut.

And just as Bryce turned on his heel and walked away, "Why would she be a vegan when she's a Christian?!" I spat. "That makes no sense."

Bryce turned around, mouth flapping but saying nothing. He stood against a shelf of sage green books with yellow trim, and I couldn't help myself, I thought, my, he looks so tanned and handsome against that sage green binding.

"You know what's *really* disrespectful?" he said, jabbing two fingers in the air. "It's not only the disrespect you're showing me and our three—and—a—half year relationship with this *outdated, misguided, unChristian* idea of what you think God wants."

We should buy him a suit that colour, I thought, it's really making his usually dull hazel—coloured eyes sparkle and even pop!

"It's the disrespect you're showing two of the world's great religions by opening the pages of a book about them, and slapping a piece of bacon between them."

My chin trembled.

"And you know Jews and Moslems don't eat fucking bacon." His eyes flashed and his jaw clicked and he added, "Even *you're* not that stupid." And he slid down to squat on the floor, his head cradled in his hands.

The only sound I heard was my footsteps on the floor. I stood over Bryce and opening up *The Jews of Moslem Spain, Volumes 2 and 3* by Eliyahu Ashtor, slipped out the bacon rasher.

"Here sweetie," I whispered, waving the bacon in front of his hands. "I think you need this more that Beatrice."

He looked up at me with red eyes, and sniffed.

"I don't like bacon," he said. "It's too fatty and too salty."

How I Displeased
the Vegans

Michael Gigandet

When my children were young I used a special strategy to counter their protests at the dinner table: the psychology of irritation.

When one of them announced that he did not like his potatoes or carrots or pork chops, I'd shout "Good! More for me!" and tuck into my portion, murmuring "hmmm" and "hmm, hmm, hmm" as I ate. When I finished I'd say, "Boy o boy I think I'll have some more potatoes!" It drove them crazy. (I was younger then and did not have to worry about calories. Retired 60–something lawyers must exercise some restraint, so if any of my children ever gets around to producing some grandchildren, and assuming that they ever visit so I can torment them, I'd have to restrain my enthusiasm at the dinner table and find another way to deal with their food complaints.)

Thankfully, and despite having me as a father, my children became healthy American citizens, avid consumers of carrots, potatoes and pork chops. Psychology works that way; you can't always explain it.

My enthusiastic retort did not go over as well in the lunchroom of Overton, Hill and Hood, the law firm in Nash-ville where I was a trial attorney for 35 years. The increasing number of vegans who joined our legal staff through the years did not appreciate our enthusiasm for meat, milk and eggs and could get downright sensitive about it.

Somebody was always bringing food into the office lunchroom to share, especially cakes and pies and pizza. One paralegal, a woman named Harper who never combed her hair as far as I could tell, was a vegan and she would always say something like: "Does it have eggs in it? I don't eat eggs." Or, "Do you use milk in your baking? I don't drink milk."

The first time it happened I couldn't stop myself. It just came out: "Good! More for me!"

Vegans don't appear to have any sense of humor at all; Harper and her associates didn't.

"I don't eat anything with a face!" Harper declared.

"Funny," I said. "I won't eat anything that couldn't defend itself if it wanted to." (That isn't exactly accurate. I've never had to stalk and subdue a carrot or a potato.)

You know who else did not have a sense of humor? Hitler. He was a vegan too, and he liked to tell his dinner guests all about it.

Surprisingly, Hitler and his cronies were also big animal lovers.

(*Mansplaining* is permissible if your intention is to irritate someone. P.S. Mansplaining is not a real word.)

Actually, I told them, the Nazis enacted legislation which many would consider revolutionary even these 80 years later if it had been enacted by a decent society. Nazi Germany passed laws prohibiting animal experimentation, regulating the care of animals used in movies, outlawing the use of dogs in hunting; it was the first country to place the wolf under special protection and the first country to host an international animal welfare conference.

Our vegans did not like knowing any of that either.

There were times when I innocently offended the vegans. A cliché is a cliché because it is popular, and it is popular because it conveys an abstract which people readily understand.

Clichés are not necessarily bad things if communication is your objective...so, you don't necessarily consider their political implications before you utter them.

"That's my meat and potatoes," I'd say, describing some aspect of my legal practice. Or, I'd refer to a courtroom victory as "bringing home the bacon." Immediately the vegans would act all...nonplussed. Once Harper found a good, winning case for me which I could use as argument in a legal brief, and I, trying to be nice, commended her for "saving my bacon."

A case could be made that I am a victim here.

Don't ask vegans what they feed their dogs either, even if you really want to know. And, don't ask why we have canines in our very own mouths.

Speaking of dogs, I have always wondered whatever happened to Hitler's dog. She was a German Shepherd (go figure), and her name was Blondi.

Some people swear Blondi was poisoned like Hitler as the Russian army descended upon his Berlin bunker. Others say Blondi was shot. Nobody knows for certain although it seems they agree that Blondi was done in by her handlers.

Blondi did not commit any atrocities. It wasn't her fault that her owner was a monster. After Hitler killed himself, why didn't her handlers just open the door to the bunker and let Blondi run off into the rubble of Berlin? "Go! Run free!" Blondi might have survived the destruction. It isn't like the

Russians who were scouring Berlin for Hitler would recognize Blondi and mistreat her. "Hey everybody! There goes Hitler's dog! Get her!"

Vegans always own dogs and did not appreciate my views on dog ownership either (which I made up during a lunchroom opinion brawl since I really have no views).

Nature has designed dogs to survive in a hostile environment. Therefore, it is unnatural to train a dog. True service dogs I understand, but all other dogs should be free from the strictures of human influence. And it is not natural for a dog to live in a house either. If you train dogs to live in a house you are training their natural instincts out of them to conform to human standards of behavior. Dogs should live outside, I declared to the vegans. "Free as the wind!"

I suppose you could make an argument that Jesus was a vegan. I don't recall him eating meat in the Bible, just bread. I just can't picture Jesus gnawing on a turkey leg or getting down on a bacon, lettuce and tomato sandwich.

Of course, it looks like the only thing the man drank was wine. He even made wine, which reminds me of how I ran afoul of the Baptists, which is another story.

Novum Organum

Jan McCarthy

It happened in Hertfordshire. St. Alban's to be exact, because I was being taken to meet my future in—laws. It was a dank, early spring morning, and I realised as soon as I stepped out of Pete's car that I was underdressed for our three hours of sightseeing.

He'd told me what to wear because I'd never mixed with his kind of people before, but I should have realised there were adaptations I could make. I could have slung my parka on top of the cream wool suit and white silk blouse, and risked laddering my tights by wearing my boots. Could have stuck those toe—pinching court shoes on last minute. A brisk March breeze had messed my hair, but I figured I could do a reasonable patch—up job if we stopped for coffee.

Why did we arrive so ridiculously early, and on a Sunday morning for god's sake, when we normally enjoyed a lie—in and a full English? Sunday wasn't Sunday in those days without sex and a cooked breakfast. Why? Because Pete, bless him, was so terrified of his olds that we had to make sure if the car broke down we could still make it by train. Pete's folks had several hard and fast rules and punctuality was one of them. He got back from Cambridge an hour late one time, end of term, sleep—deprived, laden with books and dirty washing. The tutor giving him a lift home had been a spectacularly slow, nervous driver, so it wasn't Pete's fault. Got home to find himself locked out. Note on the front door of the cottage read: *Out to dinner. Sandwiches in shed. Back by midnight.*

I'd written the other rules down in case I forgot any of them. Stuff like whether to shake hands or cheek–peck, how to sit, what word to use for *toilet*. I was pathetically, fatally besotted with Pete Goodman. Still am, come to that. What can I say? He's handsome, intelligent, well–off and a research scientist who likes to extend his research into every crevice, if you know what I mean. He's also extremely generous. The suit, blouse, shoes, matching handbag, horsey Hermès scarf were all paid for by Pete. He'd graduated First Class and been taken on by the University, whereas I was in my final year. My parents had cut me off as soon as I'd told them I was getting married, so I was penniless. I should explain that Dad wanted me to go into the family firm, but I didn't fancy being a mortician. I have unsettling psychic abilities, you see.

So I'm on my own while Pete's gone off to buy flowers for his mother, leaving me in this church he wanted to show me: St. Michael's. It's where Sir Francis Bacon, Elizabethan statesman and philosopher, is buried. I'm sitting in a back pew, shivering and feeling sleepy, when all of a sudden I hear a voice behind me. I turn and there's this bloke in historical costume, and I take him for a guide and say *Thanks but no thanks, my boyfriend is coming to get me in a minute*, and then I do a double–take because it's the same man whose portrait's on the cover of the brochure someone shoved at me when we came in. I also recognize him from the bust at Trinity, Pete's college: the egg–headed man with the downturned mouth. He read Law there four centuries ago. The guy's wearing a tall–crown hat, triple neck ruff and quilted doublet above skinny legs in tights, same as in his portrait. He's standing behind me smiling.

I stand up, make an awkward curtsey, apologize and ask why he's hanging around here in ghostly form. Surely he should have *ascended* long since. He doffs his hat, bows from the waist and says:

"Madam, the man who stands before you is, as some of your contemporaries have correctly surmised, blessed with cosmic consciousness and has therefore found no difficulty in being in two places at once."

I'm laughing out loud, partly at the things he's saying and partly at the way he's saying them when Pete returns. My boyfriend's red in the face and clutching a bouquet of white lilies. He can't see my friend Francis. Pete's spiritual side is sadly underdeveloped. He grabs me by the hand and I just have time to wave goodbye before I'm dragged to the car.

"I was looking all over for you, darling. Why do you have to go wandering off? And what were you laughing at like a crazed hyena?"

Pete's irritable as he starts up the car. He's as white as the lilies, and his hands are tight on the steering wheel. He nervously twiddles the radio knob until I take over and find us some relaxing classical music to listen to. I think he's worried I'm going to get hysterics at his parents'. I won't. I'll be a good girl, remember the house rules and try not to think about the things Bacon told me, about the future, about the afterlife, about the spirit world. I can't tell you, because I've been sworn to secrecy on pain of haunting, but if you happen to be in St. Alban's and are feeling brave, go and sit in the back pew at St. Michael's and you never know, the great man might manifest.

If he does, tell him it'll be a while before I'm able to visit. Pete and I are in the States now and I'm eight months pregnant. Way to pin a girl down. But, while lying whale—like on the sofa, I've managed to read the whole of the *Novum Organum*, my mate Francis's masterwork. He insisted I read every word of it, and who am I to argue with a Lord Chancellor? It's been heavy going, but I've realised something. Every word of it is spot on. And what's more, the human race hasn't learnt a thing in four hundred years.

Also from Pure Slush Books

https://pureslush.com/store/

- The Beautifullest Pure Slush Vol. 17
ISBN: 978−1−925536−23−2 (paperback) / 978−1−925536−24−9 (eBook)
- The Shitlist Pure Slush Vol. 16
ISBN: 978−1−925536−90−4 (paperback) / 978−1−925536−91−1 (eBook)
- Happy^2 Pure Slush Vol. 15
ISBN: 978−1−925536−39−3 (paperback) / 978−1−925536−40−9 (eBook)
- Inane Pure Slush Vol. 14
ISBN: 978−1−925536−17−1 (paperback) / 978−1−925536−18−8 (eBook)
- Summer Pure Slush Vol. 12
ISBN: 978−1−925536−13−3 (paperback) / 978−1−925536−14−0 (eBook)
- tall…ish Pure Slush Vol. 11
ISBN: 978−1−925101−80−5 (paperback) / 978−1−925101−98−0 (eBook)

Also from Pure Slush Books

https://pureslush.com/store/

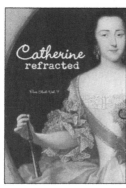 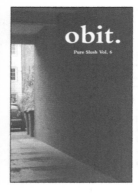 

Also from Pure Slush Books

https://pureslush.com/store/

  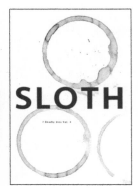

- Envy 7 Deadly Sins Vol. 6
ISBN: 978−1−925536−70−6 (paperback) / 978−1−925536−71−3 (eBook)
- Wrath 7 Deadly Sins Vol. 5
ISBN: 978−1−925536−68−3 (paperback) / 978−1−925536−69−0 (eBook)
- Sloth 7 Deadly Sins Vol. 4
ISBN: 978−1−925536−66−9 (paperback) / 978−1−925536−67−6 (eBook)
- Greed 7 Deadly Sins Vol. 3
ISBN: 978−1−925536−64−5 (paperback) / 978−1−925536−65−2 (eBook)
- Gluttony 7 Deadly Sins Vol. 2
ISBN: 978−1−925536−54−6 (paperback) / 978−1−925536−55−3 (eBook)
- Lust 7 Deadly Sins Vol. 1
ISBN: 978−1−925536−47−8 (paperback) / 978−1−925536−48−5 (eBook)

L - #0174 - 140820 - C0 - 229/152/14 - PB - DID2888225